DARK RIVER STONE COLLECTIVE #1

THE light BENEATH THE dark

JP SAYLE

JP Sayle

Copyright © 2020 by JP Sayle

All rights reserved. No part of this publication may be reproduced, distributed, or transmitted in any form or by any means, including photocopying, recording, or other electronic or mechanical methods, without the prior written permission of the publisher, except in the case of brief quotations embodied in critical reviews and certain other noncommercial uses permitted by copyright law.

Book Cover © 2020 Design by Tina Løwén

Editing by Lucas Cornelius
Proofreading by Abbie Nicole
Book Formatting by Tina Løwén

References to real people, events, organisations, locations, or establishments are only intended to give a sense of authenticity and have been used fictitiously.

The author acknowledges the copyrighted or trademarked status and trademark within the book.

Films, music, and lyrics *mentioned are the property of the copyright holders.*

Warning
Some of the content of this book is sexually graphic, with the use of explicit language and adult situations involving two males. It is only intended for mature audiences.

JP SAYLE

The Light Beneath the Dark

Lincoln Stone is President of the Dark Angels motorcycle club, and he's been accused of a crime he didn't commit. Will this finally be his downfall?

Lincoln lives a life that straddles the fine line between right and wrong. Now he stands accused of a crime that could see him losing everything he holds close and breaking a promise to the one person who loved him unconditionally, his sister.

That is, until Mason.

Mason Davenport believes in the law and what it stands for. When his father asks him to take on Lincoln's case, he learns some things are not as clear cut as they seem. Can he see beneath the exterior Lincoln hides behind to help him battle for his freedom and keep what he treasures most? Or will those who are conspiring against Lincoln win?

The Light Beneath the Dark is a standalone MM gay romance, with a sassy little girl that can offer one man freedom and another what he never realized he wanted, a daughter.

JP Sayle

JP Sayle

Tina gave me pictures and an outline and from that came this book. I hope you love it as much as I do and Tina as always you are an inspiration.

JP Sayle

Prologue

Lincoln

Bile rose up my throat as I entered the hospital and its scent invaded my senses. I'd only ever had bad experiences when I came into this place, and the hairs on the back of my neck standing up and my gut clenching, told me this time wouldn't be any different.

As I approached the front desk, the sound of my boots hitting the floor drew the attention of the sleepy-eyed woman who manned it. Her visible jerk and widening eyes were a reaction I was used to, so I kept my face a neutral mask.

"Can I help you?" Her southern drawl was filled with anything but friendliness.

"My sis called, she's havin' a baby. I'm her birthin' buddy." I rasped, and this time my lips twitched at the horror crossing the woman's face.

Her cheeks paled as her gaze roamed over me. I was sure she'd missed nothing, from my six foot five inch height, to the black leather I wore, to my long, wavy, dark brown hair I'd not bothered to brush in my haste to get here.

The call I'd gotten an hour ago from my sister to say she'd gone into labor early, filled me with dread. I'd somehow blocked out this possibility when she'd insisted on me being there for her. I'd been there for her throughout our shitty lives, and this was no different and she knew it. Even if I didn't have the first clue as to what I was doing. I mean, I'm a thirty-five-year-old tattoo artist who runs a motorcycle club. How the fuck was I supposed to be someone's birthin' buddy for fucksake?

"Her name?" the woman squeaked.

"Lizzie Stone."

The sounds of tapping filled the dead air between us and I scraped my booted foot on the floor as I glanced about, only seeing one other guy, slouched sleeping on one of the plastic chairs. A Tuesday in the hospital seemed to be a slow night. I'd have to remember that the next time I needed to come.

I hated sitting waiting for hours for some trainee to come and patch up whatever injury I'd gotten from fighting. They always gave me someone that looked like their Mamma still had to wipe their ass.

"It appears your sister is booked into the maternity ward, it's on the second floor." She pointed behind me. "Take the elevator to the second floor, turn right as you exit, and go straight down to the double doors. There's a bell to press to call for attention. They'll check with your sister before you can enter," she warned, and I rolled my eyes.

I glanced at the bank of elevators before giving her a nod. "Thanks."

In the elevator I rubbed at my eyes, trying to get rid of the tired feeling. I'd been up till one in the morning, finishing a tattoo on a prospect to the club. Quinn, aka Rattlesnake, had given me a headache as he'd whined and fucking moaned about how painful it was. Was it my fucking fault he'd chosen to have a rattlesnake tattooed from one hip bone to the other? I'd warned the stupid fuck it would be painful over bone, but he'd insisted.

I'd had a few moments of doubt, wondering whether we'd made a mistake giving him entry into the club the way he bitched, but he'd not passed out or asked me to stop, so that was something. Sid, my second in command and otherwise known as Serpent, had passed out cold the first time I'd tattooed him. He'd never lived it down, and the old crew still gave him shit for it.

The elevator chimed as it reached the second floor and, walking out of the elevator, I rolled my shoulders to ease the stiffness in my upper back from being hunched over. Turning right, I headed down the hall that smelled of disinfectant, though the scent didn't quite mask the odor of blood and guts.

The couple of people roaming the hallway dressed in dark green scrubs gave me a wide berth as my feet thudded loudly in the nearly empty hallway. The walls were painted a pale rose color and held some cheery pictures.

Reaching the door, I pressed the bell and waited, looking into the security camera.

"Hello, how can I help?" asked a tiny female voice.

"My sister rang me, Lizzie Stone. She's in havin' a baby. I'm Linc Stone, you should be expecting me. I'm her buddy to help her through this," I muttered, heat riding up my face at the silence that followed. I'd bet my last dollar the woman was probably comparing me to my tiny sister, with her angelic face. People often questioned our relationship until they looked at our eyes. The deep brown was threaded with gold and, depending on mood, could look more gold than brown.

It was the only good thing we'd gotten off our Pop. Mercifully, the mean ass fucker was long gone, so wouldn't get anywhere near this new baby to spread his hate.

"I'll need to check before I can let you in."

The tiny voice pulled me from a place I didn't really want to go and I watched the light above the camera go out. I stood like a dick, kicking at the floor. Why had I agreed to this?

The issue was, I'd do anything for my baby sister and she knew it. She had conned me when her fly-by-night ex had done a runner. What I should have done was chase his deadbeat ass down and hung him up by his balls until he agreed to support her. What did I do instead? Said yes to this madness.

That's why I'm here in the middle of the night, getting ready to tell her to breathe, and avoid looking at her pushing a tiny human out of her body!

What the fuck was I thinking?

Blaming the warmth in the hall for the sweat gathering around my hairline, I took off my leather jacket, leaving me in just the short-sleeved T-shirt I'd dragged on after the call. I glanced down and didn't get a chance to swear when there was a buzzing sound and the door was released. With a sweaty palm I opened the door, dragging in a deep breath to try and slow down my thundering heart.

The Killer T-shirt I wore was forgotten about as I walked down another long hall, this one in a deeper pink, past several open doors. Some rooms were empty, while others housed heavily pregnant women and what I assumed were their folks to help.

I pushed aside the fact I probably looked as terrified as some of the faces I'd seen. By the time I got to the desk, the one member of staff I'd seen initially as I'd started the long walk had morphed into five. I got the feeling whoever had answered the intercom had called their buddies to come and get a good look at me.

Belton, Texas has a relatively small population, around twenty-three thousand, and our motorcycle club is well known, if not for all the right reasons. It didn't stop the folks from coming to use the auto shop I owned to get their vehicles fixed, or to the tattoo shop I had to get inked. We paid our taxes and, on the whole, kept our noses clean...sort of. None of that made a difference to some of the folks though, who thought all bikers were just bad news.

I swallowed a sigh and tried to keep from scowling. "Lizzie Stone, where is she?" There was the sound of a loud mewl, followed by several cuss words I'd have been proud of, as a door opened behind the desk. Holy fuck, what were they doing to the woman?

Icy dread ran through me as I recalled Lizzie's insistence that I watch a few of the birthing videos on YouTube. The 'hell no' I'd stuck to might not have been the best idea.

What was I walking into? Right then, I'd have preferred running into a rival motorcycle club on my own, rather than facing what was about to happen.

"If you'll follow me, I'll take you to the birthing room. Lizzie has just been taken in. I'm Anne-Marie and I'll be the midwife assisting with the birth—"

"How the fuck can you be assisting if you're standin' here," I ground out harshly.

She took a step back, her face flushing rosily. "Erm…well…I was waiting for you," she stuttered, sounding flustered.

"Then you better get movin'." For some reason I couldn't explain, a sense of urgency took hold of me. I never gave the other women a thought as I met Anne-Marie's unprofessional glare.

"What're we waitin' for?" I raised the hand not holding my jacket and indicated she should get moving.

She swung around and huffed loud enough for me to hear, but I didn't give two fucks. The sense of unease I'd had from the moment I'd answered my phone was increasing by the second. I wasn't sure if it was just the reality of what was about to happen, or something else, but I'd always listened to my gut and it was saying 'get movin'.'

Anne-Marie led us back down the hall to a double door that required a security swipe to enter. The scent that hit my nose as we walked through was like nothing I'd smelled before, and I started to breathe through my mouth, not wanting to think about what it was.

We came to yet another desk, a woman in navy blue scrubs sitting at the computer. She looked up and I gave her ten out of ten for showing no reaction as her gaze swept over me, before going to Anne-Marie.

"Anne-Marie, I thought you were bringing Lizzie in?" Her tone was sharp and her eyes held a hint of steel.

"I was waiting for her brother. Stop fussing, Barb, I'm here now."

Something passed between the two women I didn't understand, but it felt off. I shook it off as Anne-Marie went to the door on her left and opened it. The cry of agony coming from my sister left me in a cold sweat and I was running through the door ready for battle. I stopped cold at the sight before me.

Anne-Marie chuckled and tapped my shaking arm as she passed by me, letting the door close behind her. "It's perfectly normal for Lizzie to be making these noises."

I didn't hear a word she said as I took in Lizzie. Her Stimpy pj top stopped at her bloated waist, revealing her bare ass. The back of the gurney she was on had been raised so she could hang on to it as she knelt. There were several sheets beneath her naked bottom half, covered in blood, and god knew what else, as it ran down her legs while she rocked, mewled, and cried out in distress. She seemed to repeat the pattern of rock, mewl, and cry.

The urge to run the other way was forced away by the need to make it all better, to stop what was hurting her. I felt utterly useless because this was a foe I couldn't fight. I threw my jacket onto a small two seater sofa in pale blue that was off to the side, taking a steading breath as I walked to Lizzie.

"Lizzie? Lizzie, I'm here baby girl, I got you." I avoided looking down at her lower body as I stroked her back as she'd taught me to do. Firm but not too firm. Her words ran through my head as she twisted to look at me.

Her eyes were full of tears and had black circles around them. Her skin was sweaty, and her long dark brown hair was stuck to her forehead.

"Oh thank god you're here. Help me Linc. Make the pain stop. Something's wrong, I can feel it," she cried, ripping at my heart with her anguish.

Her body rippled under my hand as I continued to stroke her. I glared at Anne-Marie, who was talking to the other woman wearing a set of pale lilac scrubs, paying Lizzie no attention. "Do something, she says somethin' ain't right."

"Now everything is fine. This is just part of birthing. The mom can get a little upset."

She got no further when Lizzie cried out, "I wanna pushhhhhh."

Anne-Marie came over and tutted. "You've only been laboring for a couple of hours. This is your first birth and it can take several hours before you'll feel the need to push."

Her tone sounded condescending to me, but as I was clueless, I bit my tongue.

But Lizzie was having none of it. "I'm tellin' you I need to fuckin' push," she panted, and took hold of my other hand, holding it in a death grip. "Make them do something," she pleaded with me after she got her breath back from another contraction.

Her whole body seemed to be alive the way it rippled and contracted. My knees weakened when I looked down between her legs and saw a pool of congealing blood. Back to breathing through my mouth, I glanced back at Anne-Marie, who didn't seem at all concerned.

Then all hell broke loose as Lizzie screamed so loudly I thought she'd burst my ear drums and the two women ran to the bed. Anne-Marie finally examined Lizzie and when she stood, her face showed real fear.

"What's wrong?"

She didn't answer as she hit the emergency buzzer at the back of the bed and people started to appear like ants coming out of the woodwork. They were everywhere. Lizzie held onto my hand, her eyes pleading with me to help.

"Can someone tell me what the fuck is going on?!" I roared to the room, my fear fully in charge.

The woman who'd been sitting outside at the desk stated, "We have no time to waste, the baby is stuck. The shoulders are wedged in your sister's pelvis, we need to get the baby out..." she trailed off as a man entered the room and she started to relay information to him, ignoring me completely.

I lowered my head to Lizzie's, my hair curtaining her face to keep her from seeing the chaos in the room. "I'm here, I'm gonna keep you safe, I swear." Even as I said it, I could see resignation fill her face with a knowledge I couldn't even fathom.

"Keep River safe. Promise me no matter what, you'll keep my baby safe. I've signed all the legal guardian paperwork and registered it with the court, so you won't have any issues." Her voice faded as her color drained. Her body went rigid and another scream froze my insides. This was followed by the cries of a baby.

"Come on Lizzie, you've got a baby to care for, stop this shit," I rasped through the ball of emotions clogging my throat. Her eyelashes fluttered and her hand went slack in mine.

Chapter 1

Five Years Later

Linc

The blonde who'd just sat down in my tattooist chair discussed with her friend where best to place her first tattoo. At the same time, she batted her fake eyelashes at me, like it was a sexy thing to do. She looked like she'd stuck dead spider legs to her eyes and there wasn't anything sexy about that.

Her friend wandered over to the wall, oohing over the designs I'd done and deemed suitable for photographing and displaying for folks to see what I was capable of. "This one here is stunning. The letters are calligraphy, right?" the blonde's friend asked.

I didn't look at the wall because I knew every picture. There was only one with calligraphy writing and it was tattooed over my heart. I blinked and took a steadying breath as the grief I'd never dealt with rose to remind me of what I'd lost when Lizzie died.

"Oh Tiss, you'll have to get your tattoo displayed—"

"That wall is only for big pieces of artwork," I stated, probably more harshly than was needed, shutting down any thoughts that Tiss would get her unimaginative butterfly on my wall of art.

Tiss sighed and went back to doing the fluttery thing with her eyes. "Linc, you know you'd love my picture up there." She giggled like I'd made a stupid mistake as she eyed me from head to toe and licked her slick lips, and I was reminded that she'd applied to be a prospect of the club.

I exhaled gustily at her total lack of subtlety. "Did you decide where you wanted the tattoo?"

Her small hand moved to the shoestring strap of her top and she gave me a smile that had far too many teeth in it. "I'm thinkin' the top of my boob. I'm told they're my best asset." She tugged the top over her perky, tanned boob, just shy of revealing the nipple.

Fuck, where did they learn this shit? I'd tan River's ass if she ever pulled this kind of shit when she grew up.

I nodded, then went to wash my hands and grab a pair of gloves. I was ultra-careful with my clients and my equipment. I'd been checked out so many times by the cops because of who I was, I took no chances. The friend took a seat in the corner and chatted as I placed a cover over the half exposed boob, being careful with where I touched.

Cleaning Tiss's skin with alcohol spray, I waited for it to dry before placing the design I'd drawn up with her specific requirements onto her skin. The only decent thing about doing this tattoo was the color choices I'd lined up to use. When I was happy with the placement of the outline, I picked up my tattoo gun. The buzz from the gun was drowned out by the music drifting from the shop below.

Nutty, my right-hand woman, ran the shop and arranged the bookings for me and the three other tattoo artists I employed. She also kept the bookkeeping ready for the accountants. It had been the reason I'd taken her on, she was a whizz with figures. She managed them for the club, the auto shop, and the tattoo shop. If I needed any information, she could have it with just a couple of clicks.

She was also head over heels in love with Troy, one of my tattoo artists I'd employed a couple of years back. Only thing was, she didn't have the right equipment for Troy. He didn't flaunt his sexuality, but one gay man could spot another. As I didn't talk about my business either, I'd just had a quiet word in Nutty's ear, trying to let her down gently. She had a place in my protective circle and I'd do anything to make sure she never got hurt.

Voices floated upstairs as the music was lowered and my lips twitched at hearing Ali tell Nutty to turn down the racket. Troy and Ali were based on the lower level so they had to put up with her music choices. It was why I'd chosen the upstairs when I'd bought the house five years back and converted it into River's Tattoo shop.

Kyle, one of the other artists, had opted to take the room next to mine because he also liked to listen to weird shit while he worked. He often complained that Nutty's choices messed with his vibe. Kyle's room was empty this week as he'd gone to visit with his folks, leaving me free from having to block out two kinds of music. It had been bliss these last few days, not that I'd say anything to piss off either Nutty or Kyle. They weren't just great employees, they were extended family. A family I could trust to have my back through the darkest of times.

My jaw ached as I again worked not to think about the past. *The past is the past.* That phrase went on to replay as I worked to complete the uninspired butterfly Tiss was giving herself as a twenty-first birthday present.

The outline of the tattoo was something clients struggled with, especially if it was their first. Tiss started to squirm and I gave her a warning glare that made her still. All my clients were warned to not fucking move or it could fuck up the design. It was the thing I hated most about tattooing, the repeatedly unprepared. Why do people think a tattoo won't hurt? I'm going to stab their skin with a needle for long periods of time. Unless the person is a pain slut, that shit won't be pleasant.

Her sweet scented breath hit the side of my face in fast puffs. I lost myself in the design and the perfection of the art. Regardless of what I thought of the design, I gave my all when it came to inking anyone's skin.

I'd spent nearly two decades honing my skill. The six-month waiting list for appointments showed that even if I was a bad boy, people were still willing to plonk their ass in my chair and have me ink them. Hell, some fuckers traveled from out of state for the privilege of having one of my unique designs inked on them.

The hour flew by, and by the time I was finishing up, it was evident Tiss was more than ready for me to stop. I eyed her waxy looking face and the tight line of her mouth.

"You okay?" I only asked because the last thing I wanted was for her to faint on me.

"Yeah…I'm glad it's over though." She looked at her friend. "Your turn next, Bee."

"Nah, I never booked a spot. I thought I'd wait to see how you did," Bee responded, sounding relieved to not be the next in my chair as she strolled over to take a closer look.

I cleaned the blood off Tiss's red and inflamed skin, explaining the care required for the next week while I dressed it. When I was finished, I disposed of my gloves and followed a slightly unsteady Tiss and Bee down the stairs.

"I'll grab you a set of written instructions before you leave—"

The door burst open and hit the wall, causing the top piece of glass to shudder in the frame and me to stop talking.

Three law enforcement officers came through the door and my whole body tensed at what it meant when they eyed me. Instantly, I knew they'd come for me, but I had no clue what it was I'd supposedly done this time. I gave them a toothy smile and leaned on the counter I'd gone behind to get the instructions. Nutty remained silent, but her hand reached for mine and gave it a squeeze of reassurance.

"What can I do for you, officers?"

"You can come quietly, Lincoln. We need you to come with us to the Bell County Sheriff's Department to answer some questions. There's been a serious allegation made against you," Sheriff Cranford answered with smug satisfaction.

He rarely got off his ass to leave his office, but he and I had a long history going back fifteen years. When he'd been appointed as Sheriff, he'd taken it upon himself to run the riffraff out of town. The riffraff being the Dark Angels motorcycle club that had been set up by my granddaddy. He'd died when I was young and I couldn't remember him, but I'd heard great things about him from some of the older club members.

The townsfolk used our businesses, but on the whole, kept their distance. I was convinced the folks avoided us so as not to get drawn into Cranford's hate campaign. He also liked to lord it over the town and the council. He was a total dickwad, full of his own importance, who hated that I'd not gone anywhere. It had worsened when my businesses had thrived, even with his constant harassment for the slightest infractions.

I'd been born and raised in Belton, and my family went back generations. The only way I'd be leaving was in a box, and I'd made that more than clear to him.

I eyed the two deputies as I came around the counter. The younger, blond one, Milton, put his hand on his gun and I rolled my eyes at him.

"Are you arresting me?" I growled, putting as much menace into my voice as I could.

Milton's hand trembled, although he didn't back up. The other deputy, I couldn't place him so assumed he was new, eyed me, revealing nothing. I moved closer to them, then noticed the wide-eyed Tiss and Bee watching the show.

I swallowed a curse, knowing that it would be all over town before I got to the Sheriff's office.

"Nutty, can you give Tiss the instructions and take her money. Cancel my clients for the day." I didn't glance at Nutty but looked straight at Cranford. "I take it I won't be back today?"

The grin that crossed his face caused my stomach to knot. It was full of glee like he had a dark secret. "You'll be lucky to have a business to come back to by the time you get out, boy."

His condescending tone was nothing new, but the guy with Cranford looked more than a little alarmed by the unprofessional behavior.

"Nutty, there should be a number in my book out back for a lawyer based in Killeen, Steven & Davenport. Ask for Mr. Davenport and tell him I need a lawyer. You know what to do about River." I kept all the emotions riding through me locked down as I was led away like a criminal, giving the quiet neighborhood yet another show at my expense.

JP Sayle

Chapter 2

Mason

"Oh, I'm glad I caught you Mason," came a deep voice from the doorway.

I glanced up from the desk I'd been tidying to get ready to go to court. "Yeah, I was just getting ready to leave. Can whatever it is wait? It's Judge Olsen and you know he hates it if you disrupt his golf plans for the afternoon."

My father came fully into my office, chuckling. His feet moved silently over the thick plush carpet. His suit was navy, as was his tie. The white shirt showed off his tan. It still shocked me some days that his hair was now full grey and there were deep lines around his eyes. He continued to keep his athletic body through some punishing work outs that I avoided because I wasn't stupid.

His military background was evident in the way he stood, as if he was getting ready to salute a commander. A niggle of regret wormed its way past my defenses. Defenses I'd built to stop the remorse I felt at not doing as he'd wanted and follow him into the military like my brothers. It didn't matter that he'd not once said he was disappointed. I could see it on his face, hear it in his voice when he talked about my brothers. I consoled myself that I'd gone into law and joined the practice he'd started when he'd left the service, though it made little to no difference when the feelings of failing him crept up on me.

"I need to ask a big favor. Do you remember a few years back when I took on the case of Lincoln Stone, head of Dark Angels motorcycle club? The man whose sister died tragically during labor in Belton."

I twirled a pen between my fingers, a habit I'd developed when I thought about something important. "Yeah, didn't the baby get stuck inside the pelvis? Shoulder dystocia caused a uterine rupture and she bled to death if I remember correctly, right in front of Mr. Stone." My heart bled for what the man must have gone through, regardless of his reputation around the county. I couldn't even imagine losing a member of my family in such a traumatic way. "Wasn't there a battle over the guardianship of the child, too?"

My father's face became saddened. "Yes, I managed to sort it all out, but with his past, it was a hard battle. The sister had the foresight to register guardian status for the child. It was debated whether you could do that for an unborn infant. Some court clerk, new to the role, filed the paperwork without checking. Anyway, we managed to use that to show what the sister wanted. He got compensation from the hospital, which he used to set up a trust for the child when he became sole guardian." My father tapped at his lower lip, his expression remaining unchanged which unsettled me.

"Why are you bringing this up now?"

"I've had a call from one of his friends. It would seem that he's been arrested for rape. He's asked me to represent him again. This isn't my area of speciality—"

I held up my hand, "Dad, my caseload is already overloaded, you know this." I sounded exasperated, but I knew damn well he'd given me the back story because I was sucker for a bleeding-heart story.

"He's innocent. I know this man, for all his rough edges, this isn't something he'd do. I'd bet my whole military career medals on it. He'll be distraught at being away from River, she'll be around five years old now and without her father..." he trailed off, leaving the meaning hanging between us.

I scowled and my shoulders drooped. "Alright, I'll go and meet him, but if I don't think he's innocent then I'm sending him back to you, regardless of experience."

"Son, don't judge a book by its cover, that's all I'm going to say."

Later that afternoon, after winning my case, I was riding a high as I drove up to the Bell County Jail where I'd been informed Lincoln had been taken. The place housed maximum security prisoners, so it took nearly half an hour to get through the building to where I would meet my client.

By the time I was seated in the room they allocated for lawyers to meet with their clients, my good mood had all but disappeared. I placed my briefcase on the table that was bolted to the floor in the nondescript room that only held the table and two chairs. I pulled out the file my father had given me, but I'd had no chance to read until now.

As I skimmed through the meager information, a sense of injustice made it hard to swallow. I re-read it again, with a sinking heart at how the law could be twisted to incarcerate people with so little evidence. My blood was boiling when I heard the rattle of chains outside the door, my nerves thrumming under my skin. The door opened and my father's words ran through my mind. "Don't judge a book by its cover."

Holy fuck!

Lincoln was huge and had to be well over my six feet two. He was powerfully built and the white top and elasticized-waist pants he wore didn't detract from that. His long, wavy brown hair hung around his powerful shoulders and wasn't in the least bit effeminate. Then, I was held captive by deep brown eyes that looked as if they'd been threaded with gold. In their depths was a wealth of suffering no mask would ever be able to hide completely, and they struck at a cord deep inside me.

Motherfucker! I hated my Dad right then for playing on my sympathetic side.

This man had suffered, and it was as if he were daring the devil himself to call him out for it. The room seemed to shrink as we continued to hold each other's stare. There was a flicker of something that I recognized, and my body reacted without my permission. The look was quickly gone, and left me wondering if I'd imagined the dark arousal in his eyes as he seemed to assess and dismiss me before he'd taken two steps inside the room.

"Where's Mr. Davenport?" he rasped. His voice sounded like he'd just smoked fifty cigarettes and drunk a quart of liquor.

A shiver raced down my spine as I worked to mask my reaction to him. "I am Mr. Davenport. My father has little experience in dealing with this type of case, so he asked me to meet with you." I waited to see what he would do as he towered over me while I remained seated, working on showing him I wasn't intimidated by his aura of power. *No, I was anything but intimidated.*

"I trust your father," he paused, and scrutinized me again. His face showed nothing as he walked to the chair and sat with a bored expression.

"I'll be fine." I waved the prison guards away after they'd secured Lincoln. Only when they'd left the room did I lean forward and look him dead in the eye. "Did you rape that girl?" I asked bluntly.

His face showed respect before it went blank. "No." Truth rang out in that one word.

When he sat back, saying nothing more, it felt like he was baiting me. I opened the file, acting like he wasn't flustering me and that I hadn't already decided to defend him no matter how it would encroach into my already non-existent personal time.

"There is very little evidence in this file. All they have is the testimony of the girl that says you raped her in the clubhouse after asking her to stay behind for a drink..." A rumbling sound that resembled a bike starting startled me and I looked up from the file.

I met his gaze, only the gold seemed to have disappeared in the depth of the dark molten brown.

"It's a fucking lie. I don't get involved with club members or hang arounds. It's a hard and fast rule." He seemed to gather himself as the anger filled the small room. "She's a newbie to the club, brought by one of the other members. She got it into her head that I was going to be hers. I told her to fuck off. She didn't like that. Next thing I know I'm hauled into this shithole and accused of rape." The anger continued to buzz in the room, his body no longer relaxed. "You gotta get me outta here or they'll try and take River from me."

For the first time, I saw a chink in his armor as he struggled to keep himself under control.

"I'll work on getting you bail, first. Then we'll work to clear your name."

His chuckle was completely humorless. "You'll never get me bail, but if you get rid of the other bogus shit, that will be enough." He held out his hand toward me and I took it without hesitation. "Thanks for taking my case."

He kept hold of my hand and the warmth of his calloused palm pressed against mine felt strangely intimate as he kept my gaze.

"As long as you tell me the truth at all times, then you can thank me when I get you out of here and, how did you put it, 'get rid of the bogus charges.'"

This time there was genuine humor in the laughter. "You're alright, like your dad."

For some reason, the sentiment behind his simple words warmed me. I shook off the silly notion and released his hand to take hold of my pen with tingling fingers. "Talk me through the night she's made the allegations. I need you to tell me everything you remember."

Chapter 3

Lincoln

The clang of the chains didn't give me a moment to overlook where the fuck I was, not that I'd be forgetting any time soon. The scents and sounds of the men they housed in the County Jail they'd brought me to, kept me on high alert. There was a tension in the air that made it impossible to take five and chill. A guy needed to keep his smarts about him, and life had taught me that lesson early on. So far, I'd avoided trouble, my sheer size and 'don't fuck with me' attitude keeping most at bay. But I wasn't stupid, it would only be a matter of time before someone would want to show that they were boss.

Thing is, I didn't give a fuck who that was in here. The guys housed here weren't worth the steam of my piss. I'd fought my battles to run Dark Angels and my rep preceded me. What I didn't do anymore was look for trouble. Lizzie's death had changed that. The old familiar wound throbbed in my chest, but my chained hands prevented me from rubbing at the ache.

Was River okay? Had the state tried to take her while I was stuck in this rat hole?

It irked me more than I wanted to admit that River and I were reliant upon the dude who sat watching me with careful, sea-green eyes. There was something about him that reminded me I'd not scratched a particular itch in a long time. The smell of his cologne was spicy and expensive, and it suited him. The tug low in my belly was a distraction I didn't need or want. Besides, this sharp looking dude probably preferred his men clean cut and well put together.

His brown hair was styled short at the sides, longer on top, and brushed off his attractive face. His jaw wasn't quite square as it was a little too pointed, but his lips were full, and for a second, I indulged in imagining what they'd feel like against mine.

When his eyes narrowed on me as if I'd given away my thoughts, I slipped on a mask of disinterest, but I found my gaze shifting to the sharp looking suit he wore over what appeared to be an athletic body. How tall he was he?

Would he be able to look me in the eye when we were standing?

"Does the silence mean you've nothing else to say?"

I shifted my gaze back to his face when his honey-coated voice disturbed me. "Looks like." I kept my expression bland and worked to suppress my embarrassment. How long had we been sitting, saying nothing?

"It's too late today to petition the court for bail. I'll file first thing tomorrow, and hopefully, we'll have you out in the next couple of days. Be warned, bail might be set high and there'll be restrictions about going to the club." He continued to outline what he thought the judge would make part of the provisions for bail while he neatly placed the pad he'd used and my file into his briefcase. His tanned, manicured hands were sure and steady.

When I'd asked Nutty to contact Mr. Davenport, I had no clue he had a son that was also a lawyer. Not that we'd shared personal information other than what was necessary to sort out the shit storm after River was born. The dude had done a solid job and hadn't shown any aversion to me or the club.

After he'd trounced the hospital and made sure I kept guardianship of River, he'd given me his card saying that if I ever needed him again, he'd be more than willing to help. I'd taken him at his word. As I sat listening to his son, I wasn't so sure what all it meant that he'd sent him this time. Would the son fight as hard as his father had? I'd need to reserve judgement on that and see if he got me out of this hellhole.

Only when Mr. Davenport indicated at the glass window behind me that we were done, did the door open and I got my first chance to see him standing. He waited for the chains to be unlocked and I was allowed to stand before offering me his hand. He was a few inches shorter, but he kept his eyes level with mine as I took hold of the soft-skinned palm he offered.

"I'll check in with the court appointed official dealing with your case and ensure that River remains with"—his brow wrinkled—"Nutty, that's who you said was looking after her right now?"

My hair shifted around my shoulders as I gave a curt nod.

"I'll pop by the club and check in with them before I go home."

"They ain't at the club. I own River's Tattoo shop and my home is on the top floor, Nutty and River live there with me." On hearing the information, his face showed mixed emotions, ones that were gone too fast for me to decipher them.

"I've that address, I'll go there next." He seemed flustered for the first time as he glanced down at our still joined hands.

What the fuck was I thinking holding on to the dude's hand? I dropped it faster than I could change gears on my motorcycle. He stepped to the side, gave me a polite smile, and walked out the open door. I watched his retreating back for a moment and let my gaze lower to his ass.

"You got a thing for your lawyer?" came a gruff voice that held nothing but contempt.

The guard was a mean-eyed snake of a guy who was full of his own importance, though he barely reached the middle of my chest. I chose to ignore his comment, not deeming him worthy of my energy and stood still, waiting for them to lead me back to my cell.

"I'm talkin' scumbag."

I twisted my head a fraction till I could look him in the eye and then gave him a dismissive snort. The place had cameras everywhere, so there was no way I was going to start shit and jeopardize getting released on bail.

The other guard poked me in the ribs with his baton. "Get moving, big guy." His voice held a hint of frustration as I caught him giving the other guard a sideways glare.

There were some guards that weren't looking to start shit, whereas others wanted nothing more than an excuse to give a good ass kicking. This wasn't my first rodeo, but some players here had a lot less to lose than me.

Standing to my full height, I stared forward and let myself be led back down endless halls. The chains chafed at my ankles and wrists but I said nothing. Men of all shapes, sizes, and ages filled the cells we passed. The stench of blood, piss, sweat, and shit permeated the air and left a sour taste in my mouth that had remained since I'd stepped foot inside the place.

Five minutes later, back in my cell, I released a breath and wished I hadn't when I inhaled the stale scent of greasy food and it turned my stomach. There was no escape from it in the tiny concrete box that must have been close to the kitchen ventilation. At least I didn't need to share a cell, so there was that.

The only time I came into contact with other inmates was in the yard where we exercised. I'd been in this facility twice before, but not for more than a few hours. I might run a motorcycle club, but on the whole we tried to be law abiding citizens. It wasn't always possible when fools picked a fight and it was hard to step back and not show them they were idiots.

Our rep tended to keep people away from the clubhouse, situated near the northeast city limits, bordering the Leon River. My granddaddy had owned a large piece of land there and had built the original clubhouse so it was away from prying eyes. At that time it hadn't been more than a big wooden shack, but fifteen years ago a storm had demolished it.

I'd inherited everything at twenty-one, some four years before it became a pile of sticks. As my granddaddy had died before Lizzie was born, and he'd hated Swifty, the man his daughter, my mom, had hooked up with, he'd left everything to me, even though I was but a baby at the time. When I inherited, the vote for me to head the club had been a forgone conclusion, as I owed everything.

Swifty had objected, having taken over leadership after granddaddy had died. He was a mean piece of shit, who loved to beat on me and my sister when we were kids. He'd not been able to kick us out, so he'd made it his mission to make life as difficult as possible. The moment he'd challenged me, I'd been more than ready to give him a little of what he'd given to me and Lizzie. That fight was how I'd gotten the name Killer, not that I'd killed him, though it was close.

Fights between club members were all about fists and smarts. Swifty decided to break the code and had fought dirty, using a hidden blade he'd worn in a wrist sheath. He'd managed to slice nice and deep at my thigh before I'd taken him down. By the time I was done with him, he had seven broken ribs, a broken jaw, cheek bone, and nose. I'd dislocated the fingers on one hand, his elbow, and shoulder. He'd been squealing like a pig by the time I'd finished.

He'd sealed his own fate that night for breaking the code, and the club had turned their back on him. None of the club members had challenged me again since.

I blew out a breath and perched on the tiny bunk. It creaked and groaned under my bulk as I shifted to get comfortable on the thin mattress they classed as a bed.

The clubhouse and the members were mine, my place, my people. Now that fucking skanky whore, Nola Fink, was messing with that. How the fuck had I ended up in this position? Had I let things slide over the last few years? Should I have stopped members from bringing in possible new prospects? Again, came the question: Was this a setup?

These questions meant shit all when the horse had already bolted, and I was sitting in jail unable to find out the answers. Nola had fucking troublemaker written all over her skanky ass, and that was why I'd kept my distance. But could she have concocted this shit on her own? She was a typical hang-around trying to fuck her way up the chain of command. Or so it seemed after Sid said she'd tried it with him.

In the past, girls like her would've gotten my message of disinterest pretty quickly. Not this bitch! She'd somehow managed to follow me back into my apartment off the club. What she didn't know was that I'd had to bring River with me that night because Nutty had a date. A sliver of guilt was squashed quickly that I'd held back that information from Mr. Davenport. There was no way they were going to drag River into this mess. Will sassy ass think I'm withholding? *Of course he will!*

That didn't mean I'd change my mind, not a fucking chance in hell!

Should I have told him I'm gay?

That was a much harder question to answer with the attraction still buzzing through me. It wasn't common knowledge in the club that I was gay. Sid and several other brothers I trusted were aware. It wasn't that I gave a flying fuck what anyone thought, it was more to protect River from the bullshit that came with everyone knowing.

Where does this leave me? The clanging of the cell door opening and closing down the hall answered for me and I scowled.

From outside the cell, sounds of cat calls and guys talking shit continued and I rubbed at my throbbing temples. Mr. Davenport better get his shit together and get me out, and fast, because I wasn't sure how long it would take to break my control. The last thing I wanted to do was find out.

Chapter 4

Mason

Hunger gnawed at my stomach as I drove from the Bell County Jail to Lincoln's tattoo shop in downtown Belton. Food would have to wait until I'd made this final stop and I could find somewhere to grab a bite to eat. I gave a mournful sigh at thoughts of the marinated chicken and fresh, crisp salad I'd planned for dinner.

To distract myself from when I'd last eaten, my fingers drummed against the steering wheel as I focused on the road and the list of calls I still had to make. I'd already rung my father to pull a few strings to get me in front of a judge first thing in the morning. My key priority was to get Lincoln out of jail.

As cool as he'd played it, he'd struck me as a man ready to snap. I'd heard the comment the guard had made as I'd walked away, but I'd not heard Lincoln's response. Had I been right? Was Lincoln gay, or at least bi? When he mentioned he was living with Nutty, it had thrown me for a minute. The only background I had on Lincoln was all connected to the Dark Angels. And although there'd been some discussion about Nutty, I still wasn't able to figure out what she meant to Lincoln.

What does it matter? He's a client.

I shifted against the leather seat, my shirt sticking to my damp skin. The evening Texas sun caused the heat haze to rise and shimmer above the highway. I had the air conditioning on, but I also had the window of my 2011 BMW 1M open, it did little to cool the sweltering heat of summer that carried the hot wind blowing through the window.

The first thing I'd done was take off my suit jacket when I'd gotten into the car, but the leather seat was unforgiving after the car had sat in the baking sun for the two hours I'd been with Lincoln.

As if I'd lost the ability to think about anything other than Lincoln, the time I'd spent with him replayed over in my mind. The image of him standing in the doorway, his commanding presence, and fuck-the-world attitude weren't things to easily shift from my head.

The music playing from the speakers stopped as my phone rang and I clicked the answer button on the steering wheel. Before I could say hello my eldest brother's, Luis, voice boomed through the speakers.

"Where are you? You should have been at the gym ten minutes ago." Luis continued to bitch at me, not giving me a chance to respond. "I've got everything set up. It's taken me half-an-hour, you better not be canceling on me again."

Shit!

"I'm sorry. Blame Dad, he gave me a case—"

"It's always about a case. When was the last time you took any time for yourself?" Luis's genuine concern was the only reason I kept my cool while he pointed out my flaws as he saw them. He'd left the Army Special Forces the year before and worked from home. His CPA business had several big clients that meant he could pretty much dictate how he managed his own time.

I hoped that when I could afford to branch out on my own, that it would give me more time to do the things I secretly dreamed of. The guilt I'd held about not following family tradition and joining the military meant I'd started on the bottom rung of the law firm my father co-owned. I'd gotten to the point that I could pick and choose my cases, but it hadn't lessened the need to prove I'd made the right choice of career for me.

"I can practically hear your mind ticking. It's alright, I get it. When Dad asks, you feel the need to jump to attention. We've all been there. But you're thirty years old, at some point you need to stop letting the guilt get to you."

That was the thing with older brothers. They'd already been there so could pass on their words of wisdom. Only thing was, all four of them had done what Dad wanted. "It's easy for you to say it, you didn't disappoint him," I ground out through my frustration.

"He might have been disappointed for, like, a minute, but he got over it. You need to as well." He sighed and there was the sound of someone calling his name.

"Go on, we'll rearrange for next week." I quickly said goodbye before he could start again.

Using the directions I'd looked up, I drove down Mission Drive thinking I might have taken a wrong turn. Was the tattoo shop in this urban suburb?

As I pulled up in front of the address I had for River's Tattoo shop, I shook my head and drove my car up the large driveway in front of the modern looking three-story building. My eyes widened at the reality that the hard ass biker owned this place. Lincoln, it would seem, was full of surprises.

The sand colored brick was sedate and boring. The wrap around porch on the first and second floors was well maintained. The place was nothing like I'd expected. Tucked away in a residential area, I'd bet my last dollar that Lincoln wasn't popular with his neighbors. When I'd searched the internet for the shop, River's was the only one with hundreds of rave reviews in the whole of Bell County. Lincoln's name was mentioned in most of them.

Again, my father's words ran through my head. This man was a conundrum. Appearing to the world as one thing, but he seemed to have hidden depth. Depth that was more intriguing than I wanted it to be. *Client and possibly straight!*

The muggy evening air made the decision for me after I debated for all of two seconds about putting my suit jacket back on when I exited the car. I locked my car and walked up the drive to the front door.

There was no traditional sign to indicate it was a shop. Instead, Lincoln had River's Tattoo etched into the front glass windows. As I mounted the steps to the front porch, I noted the rainbow painted wooden table and chair small enough for a child. A smile tugged at my lips as I walked to the front door. The top pane of the glass door caught my attention and I read the inscription, *Spirit Run Free.*

What did that mean? I frowned as I searched for a bell to press. Finding two, I pressed them both, hoping Nutty, whoever she was, would be in.

It took a few minutes before I heard the sound of childish laughter and a female voice shouting from inside. The next thing, the door opened to reveal a small child. Long, deep brown hair that gleamed with health hung around a tiny elfin face that held eyes identical to Lincoln's, only these were full of curiosity. Her face had smudges of dirt over the bridge of an upturned nose. There was also dirt smeared over the front of the colorful playsuit she wore. Her tanned legs and feet were bare. The wooden floor she stood on gleamed in the sunlight, showing it had been well cared for.

"Hello." She gave me a polite smile.

"I'll tan your backside, missy. What have I told you about opening the door to strangers?" came a voice from inside, then a slightly harassed looking woman in her thirties appeared. Her face was also smudged with something that looked like flour. It appeared at some point she must have run her hands through her short black spiky hair as it was tipped with white powder, along with both hands. She was as dainty as a flower and hardly reached the middle of my chest. She wore a T-shirt and a pair of shorts that revealed slender legs.

Was this what Lincoln liked?

"How can I help you?" Nutty asked, her voice sounding anything but friendly.

I gave her my most winning smile and offered her my hand before I remembered the state of them. "I'm Mr. Davenport, the lawyer—"

"Oh, yeah, right. Come in," she said, then mouthed over River's head 'Not in front of River.'

"Thank you." I kept the smile in place and dropped my hand as I was ushered inside. River glanced between me and Nutty, clearly understanding something was amiss but not sure quite what.

"U's hiding somethin', Nutty. I's can tell. Is this about where my Poppy went?"

My brows arched. Poppy? Was she talking about Lincoln?

Nutty gave a heartfelt sigh and crouched down in front of River, looking more than a little resigned. "Your Poppy is in a little bit of trouble and Mr. Davenport is going to help us sort it all out."

River turned those big brown and gold eyes on me, and my heart went out to her when she stuck her thumb between her teeth for a few seconds. "My Poppy is good, he is. Folks are just plain mean, sayin' bad tings abouts him."

She sounded so serious, I could only nod in agreement.

She stepped around the still crouching Nutty and took hold of my hand with what turned out to be her sticky one. She tugged on it until I crouched in front of her, finding it impossible to resist those big eyes.

"What is it, River?" I asked in a soft voice.

Her other hand came up and touched my cheek as her gaze held mine. She gave me the same assessing look Lincoln had.

"Folks around here sometimes are bad." Her fingers traced over my bristly cheek. "You not bad, you have kind eyes, they looks like the green sea. Will you bring my Poppy home? I's need him 'cause I's don't have a Mommy, she died. So is important to me, I's love Nutty but she's not my Poppy."

She went back to sucking her thumb and left me struggling to blink back tears. Using the years of experience I'd had dealing with difficult situations in court, I stood and looked at the silent Nutty. Her face showed her distress. A single tear slid down her flushed cheek and dripped off her chin.

I took a steadying breath and swallowed twice before I found my voice. "I'll make sure I bring your Poppy home to you and Nutty."

Please let me keep my word!

JP Sayle

Chapter 5

Lincoln

The same mean-eyed fucker from the day before opened my cell door. I remained lying on my bunk, waiting to see what he wanted.

"Get up. It seems your fancy pants lawyer has managed to get you in front of Judge Rains." His ugly face morphed into an equally ugly sneer as he carried on. "You're out of luck, Killer, Rains hates scum like you."

I slowly rose off the bed and stood, realizing he'd used my club name. My eyes narrowed. How had he known my club name? Had this fucker applied to be a prospect of the club? There was nothing familiar about him, but that didn't mean he hadn't applied and been rejected. Could this be why he hates me?

As I raised my hand to push the hair off my face, the stupid fuck shifted back. I kept the smile inside as I stared at him, saying nothing. Silence was my biggest weapon in a place like this.

"Sit the fuck back down while we chain you," he said, his left eye twitching as another guard came in behind him.

"Geoff, you ain't supposed to open the cell without backup," the other guy muttered loud enough for me to hear.

Geoff's face resembled a ripe tomato as he glared at the other guy. His lips firmed, and he kept whatever he wanted to say to himself.

Back to walking down endless halls, I ignored the cat calls and bravado. Chains rattled as I walked up the steps to the box in the courtroom. My gaze swept the room and found the usual gawkers from the local news. Mr. Davenport stood at the front of the room, his suit today a gunmetal grey. His shirt was white, and the tie was the same color as the suit. He wore an expression of deep concentration as he spoke to a woman with dark, spiky hair that had her back to me but was very familiar.

What was Nutty doing here? Fuck, where was River? Had the courts taken her? Tension crept up my spine and my neck stiffened. Panic, that always came with thoughts of anyone taking River from me, stopped me thinking rationally.

The chains chinked together while I sucked in a few calming breaths, and at the same time, I went through the mental list of activities I'd planned for River this week. The tension eased a little as I recalled today was one of the days she spent with Mina and her brood.

Mina lived five houses down from mine and popped babies out like she was shelling peas. I wasn't sure if she was on number four or five, but she was great with kids and her middle child was the same age as River, and River's best friend. Mina was happy to have River two days a week during school vacation because I paid her with tattoos that she couldn't afford with so many mouths to feed. It helped both of us.

Working to keep my expression blank, I sat on the hard seat behind the perspex the guards led me to.

Only once I was seated did Mr. Davenport glance in my direction. He gave a nod of acknowledgment, his sea-green eyes holding mine for a second longer before he turned his attention back to Nutty.

The noises in the room made it impossible for me to hear what was being said, but Nutty nodded several times before she went to take a seat. She glanced at me and gave a thumbs up, her expression one of confidence.

She mouthed, "River's cool."

It helped ease the last of the anxiety I'd covered with a blank expression. Nutty continued to smile at me, knowing me all too well not to be offended by my lack of response under the circumstances.

My gaze moved back to Mr. Davenport, who'd walked toward a man I'd seen around town once or twice. Mr. Winter had a fancy lawyer's office on Main Street. The guy had a reputation as a shark. To me, he looked like he'd been slicked up with motor grease, an oily fucker that thought he was top of the food chain when really, he was nothing but a shrimp. Some of the club members had used him in the past for minor shit they'd been hauled in for.

I frowned. Had someone at the club told the skank to go to this greasy fucker? The sense something was off, came back.

Mr. Davenport's posture went from relaxed and easy to stiff and, although he offered his hand, it appeared to be more of a courtesy than anything else. It distracted me from my thoughts as words were exchanged before the door behind the judge's table opened.

A silence fell over the courtroom.

"All rise, Judge Rains presiding," a voice requested respectfully.

Following the command, I waited until directed to return to my seat. I intertwined my fingers in my lap to hide their shaking. To show weakness was something I loathed, but with everything that was riding on today, my body wasn't listening to reason.

There was a load of legal jargon to go through, and I zoned out. It was only as Mr. Davenport stood that I tuned back in.

"Your honor, I respectfully request bail for my client. Having reviewed the evidence, or what little there is, I see no reason as to why he cannot be released on ba—"

"Your Honor, I disagree, he raped my client. Miss Fink is at risk if he is released," Mr. Winter pointed out abruptly, talking over Mr. Davenport.

Biting my tongue to stop from shouting out, air got stuck in my chest as the two men argued back and forth until the judge interrupted.

"Enough. I've read over the file. You both have valid points." His fingers templed as he sat forward, his elbows resting on the table as he stared at both men. Then he glanced at me for the first time.

"Taking into account the rather large number of previous altercations with the law

Mr. Stone has had, bail will be set at two-hundred-fifty thousand dollars."

There were several gasps, and people muttered amongst themselves before there was a call for silence. Folks were probably thinking I'd be stuck rotting in the cell, but the club had more than enough funds to pay the bail, so I wasn't worried. For the first time in three days, I breathed easy, knowing I'd be free.

The judge continued to put restrictions on me as he talked about a tracker being attached to me that was given to all sexual predators. I didn't give a fuck as long as it got me out of this place and back to River.

When the court proceedings were over, Mr. Davenport looked up at me and mouthed. "I'll be through to see you as soon as I can clear it."

Mr. Winter walked over to Mr. Davenport and laid a hand on his arm. I tensed. What did the sleazebag want?

I watched the heated exchange as Mr. Davenport shook off the hand, his expression hard as stone as he turned his back on the other guy. If I hadn't been watching closely, I might have missed how Mr. Davenport's hands trembled as he collected the papers he'd laid on the desk he'd been sitting behind through some of the hearing.

What had the dude said to upset Mr. Davenport?

With no time to dwell on it, I was led back to the jail and taken to the room we'd met the previous day. There must have been a quicker way from the courtroom, as he was already sat in the same seat, his expression showing no emotion. His ever-watchful eyes held mine as I entered the room.

There was silence between us until I was secured to the table and the guard's left the room.

Mr. Davenport glanced at the door as the lock snicked into place, then back at me. His face morphed into a smile that seemed to light the whole room, and the tug of arousal I'd convinced myself hadn't happened the day before, buzzed with renewed vigor. Fucking hell, this was the last thing I needed.

"Right, first question. The bail, do you have that kind of money or do we need to find a bail bondsman?"

"I've cash. Y'all need to talk to Nutty. She has authority to release that kind of bread from the bank without needin' my permission." Again, I noticed Mr. Davenport's reaction, his lips pinching and smile dimming. What was wrong with him?

Leave it be, it's got nothin' to do with you.

His smile never reappeared as he talked through what was going to happen. "If everything is in place, you should hopefully be released tomorrow."

I shifted forward, pinning him with a hard stare. "Nope, don't pull that shit with me, I want out today. The bank can transfer the money, and I'll take the hit for whatever additional costs there are but get me outta here *today. You hear me*," I growled angrily. There was no way I was going to spend another night in this godforsaken place.

His sea-green eyes turned to chips of hard emerald as he leaned closer to me. His nostrils flared and a dark flush rode along his cheekbones. "Watch it. I worked my fucking ass off to get you in front of a judge today." His quiet tone held a sharp edge as his jaw thrust forward and bunched, showing the restraint he was using. He sucked in a breath before his shoulders seemed to release. "I understand your need to see River so I'll make an excuse this time, but remember, I'm on your side."

Had he just told me off?

The mad fluttering in my chest said yes, as did the sizzling anger buzzing now with the arousal. Stunned into silence, I watched him as he collected himself and carried on talking like he hadn't just chewed me out.

When was the last time someone had stood up to me? A grudging, newfound respect formed as I remained quiet and stewed over what it all meant as he explained the logistics of how to get me out of jail, *today.*

JP Sayle

Chapter 6

Mason

Dragging a hand through my hair, I leaned against my car, questioning my sanity as I waited for Lincoln to appear from inside the jail while I stood in the muggy heat of the evening. I'd, yet again, missed dinner and it was all because of Lincoln.

I groaned aloud and slouched against the hot metal as I glanced up at the colorful sky, trying to distract myself. I shut out the sounds of the late evening traffic, not that there was much. Belton wasn't as densely populated as Killeen, where my home and law practice were.

My father had been stationed in Killeen with the military. My whole family had moved there when I was about four, and it was the only home I could remember. When my father had retired, he'd chosen to stay and make it his home. Then his best friend, Donny Stephens, had offered him a partnership in his law firm, making it an easy decision.

Seeing where my head was leading me, I focused on the setting sun. The deep oranges and reds streaking the sky were a thing of beauty. When the sticky heat plastering my shirt to my skin prevented me from finding any joy in the beautiful scene, I gritted my teeth.

What the hell was wrong with me?

Not for the first time that day, I queried my own sanity, as had my personal secretary, Linda, who deserved a pay raise after what she'd put up with today. How I had managed to pull it all together and ensure that Lincoln was released today was beyond me, but I'd somehow managed to get everything to line up in order, even with Linda threatening to resign twice through the day as I'd nagged at her.

After I'd left Lincoln that morning, I'd spent the remainder of the day in the office, jumping through all the hoops. The driving force had been a set of big brown and gold eyes reminding me of my promise everytime I'd wanted to curse and say tomorrow would do. *You didn't promise to drive yourself into the ground and half starve.*

I swallowed the sigh and pushed my aviator sunglasses up my nose when I caught movement through the bars of the gates to the jail. My breath caught in my lungs when Lincoln appeared with two guards.

He towered over them, his dark hair gleaming in the fading sun. His dark eyes met mine, and I wasn't sure if it were surprise I saw before he slipped on what I was coming to think of as his 'fuck you' mask. It jarred me that I was coming to recognize his different expressions after only spending a few hours with him.

It's just because you've spent so much time in the last twenty-four hours trying to sort out his crap, that's all it is. The sentiment lacked conviction and I stood away from the car. My gaze traveled over Lincoln, my head clearly not listening to reason.

The white prison clothes were gone, and he was dressed all in black. The shirt hugged his large muscular chest and was partially tucked into the front of jeans that sat low on his, surprisingly lean, hips. I licked my dry lips, eyeing legs that flexed under worn denim. Viewing the rips in his jeans, my fingers tingled as my mind wondered what his skin would feel like.

The clang of the gates pulled me back from my runaway thoughts. I tensed as Lincoln stepped through the open gate and the guard followed, speaking loud enough for me to hear.

"Oh look, your ass bandit came to collect you."

It was common knowledge I was gay, but this was the first time I'd been called out about it so offensively to my face.

Lincoln's whole body seemed to still before he slowly twisted his head toward the guy. "You jealous? You wanna be my fuck toy?" His dark, menacing glare matched the tone of his voice as he looked the guy up and down. "You look like you'll make a great bitch."

Before I could think about it, my shoes slapped on the concrete as I ran up the sidewalk to where the men both stood, facing off.

"Enough. Lincoln, River is waiting for you." Lincoln's face kept the 'fuck you' expression as he glanced briefly at me. Seeing the fire in the depths of his eyes, I stepped between both men, feeling like I'd just stepped into a boxing ring with Mike Tyson and Mohamad Ali.

Fuck. Fuck! This was the last thing I needed after I sweated my balls off to get Lincoln out.

"It looks like you're the bitch to me," the guard sneered, not getting how close he was to losing his teeth and possibly having his nose rearranged over his face.

The tension was as suffocating as the muggy air. I placed my palm on Lincoln's chest. His whole body felt like it was vibrating under my hand, but I never took my eyes off the guard. "Have you read your terms of employment by the state? I think you'll find your behavior is classed as verbal harassment." I nodded to the other guard, who looked like he'd rather be anywhere but right here.

He wasn't alone, but I kept my cool, having learned how to play referee with my brothers for years. "You've a witness right there. If my client wanted to press charges, he could."

The guard blustered, "What the fu—"

I held up the hand not touching Lincoln to get him to stop before he made matters worse. Not that I could see how, when I could feel the weight of Lincoln's gaze boring into the side of my head.

"If I were you, I'd step back inside the gate, lock it, and get the fuck out of my face before I decide to nail your ass to the nearest wall, and not in the way you evidently want." I shifted my weight forward to make my point. "Then we'll see who the bitch around here is."

The steely edge to my voice would have impressed my four brothers. There was no satisfaction for me though, as I loathed losing my temper, but the guy had pushed my buttons. And if there was one thing I hated, it was when those in authority chose to use it as a weapon against others.

The other guard's mouth hung open, catching flies behind the dickwad. I dropped the hand touching Lincoln's chest and gave him a brief look. "Let's go," I bit out. The anger was still riding me hard as I stomped back toward my car, only releasing my breath when I heard footsteps behind me.

As I opened the car door, a wave of stifling heat came at me, and I struggled to not wilt and beg for a cold beer and five fucking minutes alone to cool off. Instead, I got inside the hot car and watched as Lincoln got in beside me, struggling to stretch his long legs out.

My humor returned as he grunted and twisted, with difficulty, to look at me. "Why'd you have to pick a matchbox to drive?"

"Hello, this is a 2011 BMW 1M, it is the unicorn of sports cars. This diminutive Bavarian barn burner is all but impossible to find in the secondhand market. It commands a premium price when you can find one. This car was injected with steroids and has three-hundred-thirty-three horsepower, I'll have you know. It also has a three-litre twin-turbo and six-cylinder engine under the hood, paired with a six-speed manual transmission. It's a beast, not a fucking matchbox," I finished with a growl.

For the first time since I'd met him, Lincoln's mouth formed into a lazy smile and changed his whole face. He went from attractive to fucking stunning in a heartbeat. I was so lost in that smile, it took a second to register that he was talking.

"—gear head. Who'd 'ave thought the uptight lawyer, Mr. Davenport, had a thing for cars." His smoky voice was full of humor and a shiver ran down my spine, even in the intense heat.

"Fuck off. I'm anything but uptight, but I'll give you gear head, and the name is Mason," I grumbled in return, secretly pleased when the lazy smile remained as he shifted back into the leather seat, reaching for his seat belt.

"You gonna turn on the engine or just sit starin' at me, Mason?"

Fuck! If I wasn't already hot and bothered, the way my name rolled off his tongue would have done it.

Starting the engine, it roared to life, and instead of answering his question, I signaled and pulled out into the street. The man threw me completely off balance. He was dangerous and I needed to remember that.

Dangerous to what?
Everything!

JP Sayle

Chapter 7

Lincoln

Why had Mason come to pick me up? What was he after?

In my world, no one did anything for anyone without a reason or a motive. *What were Mason's?*

Maybe he's just a decent guy?

I nearly snorted aloud at that as I glanced down at my lap and swallowed a sigh when my arousal continued to press against my fly. I didn't do decent guys.

The quiet between us lengthened as Mason drove toward the shop. The engine was the only sound to break the silence when I opened the window to let in some air. Closing my eyes, I blocked out the uneasy thoughts and rested my head against the headrest, letting the warm air brush over my face.

Mason. The name suited him. It was a solid name, though secretly I thought sassy ass might be more apt when he'd put the guard in his place. Why had he done that? The only guys that stood up for me were the ones I called brothers.

When had anyone chosen to stand up for me just because?

His father had.

I paid him.

That might be so, but he went above and beyond to make sure I kept River.

My heart skipped several beats as I considered what the alternative could have been for River.

For years, I'd lived as I chose, not giving a fuck about what anyone thought of me, with two exception, Lizzie, and then River. Our good for nothing father had taken off when Lizzie was only two and I was ten. Mom had sunk into the bottom of a bottle until she'd drowned her liver with it. That left us to run wild at the club, being kicked about by whoever felt like it, sharing a cramped room. I'd always been protective of Lizzie, so when Mom had died when Lizzie was five, I'd taken it upon myself to look out for her.

As we'd grown, and I'd taken over the club, she'd run a little wild up in Austin. When she'd come back pregnant and alone, I'd kept her safe. *Did you? She's fucking dead!*

Guilt choked me, along with grief, while I struggled to push it back into its box where it belonged. My hands pushed down against my thighs as I twisted my head to stare out the window. The highway whizzed by while warm wind whipped at my hair and blew around my face as I considered the possibility my luck had run out again. Was I going to lose River?

Over the years, I'd been lucky to escape having to spend any real time behind bars. One thing I'd discovered about myself over the last three days, me and confined spaces didn't work. That meant my future was now dependent on the guy driving me home. The question that seemed to be my constant companion returned. Would he fight for me?

You're gonna find out because he's all you've got!

"You hungry?" Mason asked, interrupting my thoughts.

I glanced at him, and for the first time, really looked at him. Though the dark glasses prevented me from seeing his eyes, I could see strain and tiredness etched into his face that hadn't been there the day before. "I'd kill for a pizza. La Roma Pizza and Subs are about the best you'll find around these parts. They deliver. You can eat with us if you want." It was out before I could think it over.

"Yeah, that works."

His response sounded a little breathless, and my eyes narrowed on him, but he didn't take his eyes off the road. He signaled and left the highway, and within a couple of minutes he was pulling up outside the shop.

The engine had no sooner been switched off, when the door flew open and River ran out onto the porch and down the steps. Her bare feet slapped against the wood as her ponytail bounced on top of her head. Her eyes were alight with a pure love that only a child can give, leaving me struggling to keep my emotions in check as I exited the car to go to her.

"Poppyyyyyyyyyyyyy," she cried, loud enough to wake the dead.

I laughed and knelt down on the drive, a second before she launched herself at me. I wrapped my arms around her tiny body as she wriggled against me and buried her face into my neck. It was something she'd done since she was a baby, and a wave of love that never failed to warm me flowed through me. I inhaled her sweet scent and held on to her.

A tiny hand rubbed at my chest right where Lizzie's name was tattooed. "I's missed ya Poppy." She sniffed twice before she lifted her head to look at me with tear drenched eyes. "I's gonna spank ya bottom for making me worry like's dat."

Heat spread up my neck as laughter drifted from behind me from the man who'd surely followed me out of the car. *Fucksake!*

"I'm sorry, Spirit, but—"

"Don't ya but me, Poppy. Ya says we'ves gots to be honest. Nutty's sayin' nothin' and you's been gone days and days." Her brow was deeply furrowed, and she looked so much like Lizzie it hurt my heart at the truth of her words. I'd sworn I'd always be honest with her.

"Let's go inside. Mason is hungry and so am I. I'll explain as best I can, Spirit."

Her face remained serious as she looked toward the man behind me. "I's like him Poppy. He keeps his word, so we's can trust him."

My heart skipped a beat at her words. River didn't trust easy, and I'd learned to listen to her. A child's instincts were so much more attuned than adults, and in the world I lived in, instinct was everything. *Then why didn't you kick the skanky-ass bitch out of your club?*

I cursed silently and stood, putting River onto my hip as I glanced over my shoulder at Mason. His bemused expression brought back the tug of arousal, so I looked back at the house to where Nutty was stood watching us. My eyes narrowed on her.

Her black hair was in her normal spiky style, her eyes were rimmed with dark eyeliner, her lips were bright red, and she wore a short, fitted black dress with ankle boots. "You got dressed up for me comin' home?" My brows arched as she giggled and tugged at the hem of the too short dress.

"As if you'd get that lucky. I've got a date." Her face pinked as she looked anywhere but at me as she came down the porch steps.

"Who's the guy?" I kept my voice neutral.

She scowled, and I sighed at the reality I'd not kept my concern for her hidden.

"None of your business. I thought you might like some time with River…alone." Her hips swayed as she tottered on the spiky heeled boots, her face now wearing a cheeky grin I couldn't fail to understand. "Don't wait up." She blew River a kiss and winked at me before strolling off toward her beat up old Corvette that she didn't let anyone touch.

I watched her reverse down the drive and give one final wave as she drove off.

"Poppy, come on, I's got a present for ya." River wriggled in my arms.

As I crouched, she gave my cheek a quick kiss before she jumped off me. She ran back toward the house, calling for me to hurry.

I glanced back at Mason, who remained in the same spot. "You still want pizza?" I held my breath as I waited for him to respond.

"Of course, I'm starved, and we need to talk more about what happened with Miss Fink."

"Not in front of Spirit; it's not happening," I ground out through clenched teeth. Didn't he get she was only a fucking child?

He cleared the distance between us, his jaw jutting toward me, his eyes stormy. "Give me a little more credit than that." The quiet restraint when he spoke was the exact opposite to the fire in his eyes.

We stood staring at each other for what felt like the longest minute as the sexual tension between us increased. "We ain't doin' this! It's a bad idea," I rasped past my dry throat.

He didn't pretend to not understand and gave a nod of acknowledgement that left me with a bitter taste in my mouth.

"You aren't the only one with a lot to lose. I'm your lawyer." The way he said it was as if he were trying to convince someone, only he was fooling no one, especially not me. His stormy eyes held mine for a few more seconds before he stepped around me and walked toward the porch.

I released the pent-up breath I'd not been aware I'd been holding and followed him. *He's your lawyer, nothing more.* Then why was my dick hard?

I ran my hands through my hair and thought of every nasty thing I could, keeping my eyes away from the ass in form fitting trousers.

Stop fucking looking at his ass!
It's fucking right there!
So what? You ain't gonna be touching it.
Why didn't I sound convinced?

Chapter 8

Mason

"How's the case going?"

I glanced up from the papers scattered over my large teak desk and scowled at my Dad. Today he wore the casual button-down, short-sleeved shirt and slacks that he wore to play golf. "Don't ask. That bloody club and its members are like the crypt keepers. It's like trying to get blood from a stone getting them to talk to me."

I threw the pen I held onto the desk, stood up, and pushed my seat back toward the window at behind me. I didn't look out at the blue sky or the streets beneath as I walked from behind my desk, unable to sit still and have this conversation.

Frustration ran through me, and I rubbed at my temples as I strode around the room, not really seeing it as my mind ran over the last meeting I'd had with Sid, Lincoln's second in command, at the club. "I get they're a tight knit bunch and they don't take well to authority figures, especially those connected to the law, but I'm trying to keep Lincoln's fucking ass out of prison." I refused to acknowledge how peeved I sounded.

Hearing my Dad chuckle, I glanced at him, my eyes narrowing on him as I pointed out, "This is your fault. I should kick the case back to you. You can deal with that hot-headed bunch of assholes." I meant it. They'd given me nothing but a headache. On top of that, I already had an overflowing caseload I was trying to cram into as many hours of the day as I could. I'd not had a moment to myself since I'd picked up the case two weeks prior.

A look of concern crossed my Dad's face as he came toward me and took hold of my shoulders. The searching stare was followed by a deep frown appearing on his forehead.

"Are you burning the candle at both ends?"

I shook off his hands. "The chance would be a fine thing. I've been burning the midnight oil at the club trying to get witness statements from the other members for the night in question." My gut churned at how it gave me the opportunity to gain insight into all the different sides to Lincoln, Poppy, or as his club members called him, Killer. I'd not seen him since the day after we'd shared pizza as he wasn't allowed anywhere near the club.

That evening, having supper with him and River, he'd shown a soft side that I'm sure few would believe was there. His reputation was that of a mean-tempered biker that didn't tolerate fools. Yet, River held his heart, and the fierce love he had for her left me even more conflicted. I'd never thought about family and having one of my own. After I'd left them, I'd had this overwhelming need to feel a part of something that special, and I couldn't shake it.

Then I'd gone to the tattoo shop the following day, and there was the bad ass biker that had an aura that kept men wary and the women fawning all over him. I'd had to turn away from the sight more than once. It was hard to acknowledge that I was pissed after Linc had laid it out that nothing would happen between us. I'd seen no point in pretending I'd not felt the sexual tension between us. And though I'd already made my mind up that nothing was going to happen, it was still disappointing in ways I'd never felt before.

"Is there something else going on here that I'm missing?"

I exhaled gustily and looked into my Dad's probing gaze. With his years in the military and then as a lawyer, he was great at reading people, which is why I trusted his judgement. I worked to mask my thoughts as I tried to figure out how to answer without giving too much away.

"I just need a couple of days off. You know, relaxing and doing nothing but lazing in the sun rather than running around in it." That at least was the truth, the past two weekends I'd spent going over files and testimonies, trapped inside.

"Then why don't you come over this weekend for the Fourth of July celebrations? I mentioned it a few weeks back, but you didn't commit. Your brothers are all coming."

The concern was back, as was the guilt at not wanting to be around everyone and feel like the odd man out. It had worsened over the last decade when Dane, who was a year older than me, made the decision to go into the Navy, leaving me the only one not following in our father's footsteps.

I found myself agreeing as his eyes creased and a look of disappointment replaced the worry. "I'd completely forgotten it was coming up on the Fourth. It will give me a good excuse not to work. Tell Mom I'll bring my special cheesecake."

The smile that lit his face helped to unknot my stomach. "She'll be thrilled. But make sure to bake enough to feed the neighborhood. I'm sure she's invited them all!" He gave a wry chuckle as he rolled his eyes at me.

"You love it."

"I suppose I do. I miss having my boys around me," he said in such a despondent tone that I wrapped my arms around him and gave him a hard hug.

Stepping back, I nudged him toward the open door. "Go on, I see you're dressed for golf while some of us have a desk that's groaning under the strain of all the work piled on it."

"Privilege of owning your own business," he quipped back.

"Yeah, yeah." I took my seat as he strolled to the door and looked back at me.

"If you ever want to talk about what's bothering you, I'm here."

I sighed and blinked back the sudden rush of tears, blaming them on being overtired. "Thanks, Dad."

He thankfully didn't point out the catch in my voice as he gave me one final look before leaving as quietly as he'd entered.

I laid my forehead down on the pile of papers on my desk and sucked in several deep breaths as I gathered myself back together. *You're just tired is all.*

"Lincoln, I'm already running late for where I'm supposed to be. Why do I need to come to the shop?" I complained into the phone I'd tucked into the crook of my neck as I lifted the huge tray out of the refrigerator.

I hunched, trying to keep hold of the phone with my shoulder and cheek while I looked for a countertop close enough to lay down the triple-sized Nutella cheesecake I'd made for the celebration today.

"This ain't my idea, it's River's, and she won't stop pesterin' me."

He sounded pissed as his smoky voice filled my ear. My body reacted as a shiver raced over my exposed skin. A grin tugged at my lips even as I blew out a frustrated breath. I eyed the cheesecake and considered my options.

"Do you and River like burgers and Nutella cheesecake?"

"Does a bear shit in the woods? What kinda stupid question is that?" he growled, sounding confused and causing another shiver to ripple over my already pebbled flesh.

"Do you have plans for today? If I drive to Belton, the cheesecake I've slaved over will melt in the heat. It's hotter than hell out there today. So, I'm proposing—"

"You proposing to me? It's a bit soon for that," he fired back so fast my mouth dropped open at the humor in his voice.

Had he just made a joke at my expense?

A flare of heat spread up my neck and I was glad I was alone. "You're cracking me up," I quipped back, and his bold laughter left me feeling more than a little flustered. In the time I'd spent with him, his guard had remained firmly in place unless he was with River. I berated myself for feeling way more pleasure than was sensible, knowing he could be that way with me when he so rarely did it with others.

"What I'm suggesting is that you bring River to my…well actually, to my parents' home. You can have a burger and cheesecake as a reward, then explain what it was you wanted."

There was utter silence on the other end of the phone, so I pulled it from my ear to check I'd not accidentally cut him off. Seeing that we were still connected, I went over what I'd said. "Is there a problem?" I asked in a strained voice when I put the phone back to my ear and Linc remained quiet.

"You're invitin' us to your parents' home?"

"Yes, that's what I said. Is there a problem with that?" I blew out a frustrated breath, trying to see what his issue was.

"Folks don't normally invite the likes of me into their home..." There was a sound of scratching as he trailed off, as if he were embarrassed by the admission.

"I'm not folks. So, are you coming?" I held my breath and waited for his answer, realizing just how much I wanted him to say yes.

"I'm not sure that's a good idea—"

"You know my Dad," I quickly reminded him. "This isn't an issue unless you make it into one." I countered, hating the desperate edge to my voice while my palms became sticky with sweat.

"Say yes, Poppy. I wanna see Mason," came River's voice in the background.

He sighed and all I could think about was how to reward River for helping me out.

"Give me the address."

He sounded anything but happy as I gave him the address and told him I'd see him there before hanging up quick smart so he couldn't change his mind. I dropped my phone onto the counter as my hands trembled.

What was I doing?
Playing with fire!
I hesitated before picking my phone back up and, with a resigned sigh, I dialed my parents to explain they'd be having extra company.

JP Sayle

Chapter 9

Lincoln

I tugged off my shorts and pulled on a pair of jeans to hide the tracker attached to my ankle. I gave the plain navy T-shirt a passing glance as I fastened the button fly. What had I been thinking to agree to this?

"Poppyyyyyy, I's need help," River shouted from her bedroom down the hall. The little sneak was why I'd ended up agreeing to this. *You keep believin' that!*

I'd not seen her come into the kitchen while I'd been on the phone, at her request, to invite Mason over for a barbecue. That had been bad enough, but now I was going to have to mingle with folks that would probably look down their noses at me and River.

I pulled on my boots and stomped up the bare wooden floor. My boots hit the wood hard enough to make the picture frames on the wall rattle.

"You's can stop dat, we's going Poppy. I's like him. You's do to, I's sees the way ya smile at him," she stated when I stopped in her doorway.

How the fuck could a five-year-old figure out this shit when adults couldn't? I swallowed the sigh and asked, "What do you need help with, Spirit?"

I wasn't sure when I'd started calling her that, but she often reminded me of Lizzie and how free spirited she'd been, so it seemed natural to call her Spirit.

Now, as she danced around doing a full twirl to show off her dress, my heart ached for what Lizzie was missing out on. The pink summer dress with tiny daisies on it flipped out before settling around her brown legs. On her feet she wore a pair of pink, sparkly jelly shoes. Her hair was braided and hung down her back. "Is dis ok for a party, Poppy? Does I look pretty?"

"You look beautiful, just like your Momma when she was your age." I glanced over to the wall above her overly fussy pink bed. A massive picture frame with a collection of pictures of Lizzie as she'd grown up covered a large expanse of the wall.

I pointed to the one of Lizzie and me when she would have been the same age as River. "See, your Momma might not have had a pretty dress like you, but she still was beautiful." The grief cut deep, but I kept my voice steady as I ran a hand over the top of her head, needing the connection.

"She was Poppy. I looks like her, don't I?" There was a touch of sadness in her voice, so I crouched in front of her and pretended to look at her face.

I scratched my bristly chin, then flicked the tip of her nose. "You're like two peas in a pod."

She rubbed at the end of her nose and gave me a stern look. "No peas, Poppy, they're yucky." She gave a dramatic shiver before grinning at me. "Are's we going? I's ready."

Seeing no way out of it, I let her tug on my hand as I stood.

Outside, River eyed my Harley I'd pulled out of the garage and then down at her dress. Her mouth set into a stubborn line I often saw in the mirror. "What?"

"I's not getting on there, Poppy. I's not messin' me hair or getting bugs on me dress."

She sounded so horrified that I struggled not to laugh. "But you love my bike," I pointed out, already seeing it was a lost cause but needing to try and act like I was still the boss.

"Dat's right, but I's a lady goin' to a party, Poppy. I's can't go all messed up. Well, dat's what Mina says when she gets dressed up to go out and doesn't want to go on Joe's motorcycle."

This time the laughter wouldn't be stopped as she looked at me as if I was being ridiculous for even suggesting she get on my Harley, which she loved to ride with me. I wiped at my eyes and wheeled the motorcycle back into the garage, resigned to taking the truck I hardly ever used.

Once she was buckled in, I went to retrieve the present she'd made for Mason and the box of fireworks River insisted I take as a gift. The plan was to go and do what was needed and get out in the fastest time.

With that firmly fixed in my mind, I drove the twelve miles to Killeen. Although the place was close, I didn't tend to visit, with it being a military town that I had no interest in. On a positive note, Killeen did generate a lot of business for both the auto's workshop and my tattoo business.

If I went anywhere, it was usually up to Austin. It was far enough away that people didn't tend to know who I was, so I could pick up a guy, scratch an itch, then head home without shitting on my own doorstep.

It had worked that way for years, and I had no intention of changing that, no matter how attracted I was to Mason. I'd have planned a trip to Austin by now, but with the tracker on my ankle, it made it difficult to get naked without explaining shit that I didn't want to talk about.

There were already enough whispers getting back to me about what Nola had been mouthing off about. It hadn't started to affect business, *yet,* but I wasn't stupid. If this shit didn't get taken care of, and soon, then it would only be a matter of time before it would hit financially.

I'd talked to Mason two days before about taking a step back from the shop and letting the guys take my bookings. Kyle could more than match my skill, if not my flare for design. Mason had been adamant that I should carry on as normal.

"Poppy, u's ok? Ya making gruntin' noises," River asked in a serious tone.

I glanced at her and gave a smile I hoped looked real before looking back at the highway. "I've just got a lot on my mind is all. Nothin' for you to worry about, Spirit."

"I's not worried, Poppy. Mason says he's gonna keep ya safe."

The utter conviction in her words struck at the walls protecting my heart, and for a brief second, I let the belief that Mason could keep me safe slip past the barrier.

Get over yourself, the only person you can rely on is you!

Several minutes later, I pulled into a neighborhood similar to the one where I lived. I parked on the busy street just down from the address Mason had given me. I exited the truck and went to help River out of the cab. Once she had her present, and I had the box of fireworks tucked under my arm, I took her hand and headed up the sidewalk toward the house.

I wasn't sure what I expected, but I relaxed a little at seeing the house wasn't some big grand deal but more similar to my own house. We'd reached the end of the path when the door burst open and a little boy of a similar age to River ran out squealing with laughter, quickly chased by Mason.

Having never seen him in anything other than a suit, I found myself staring. His green T-shirt was soaked, as were the beige cargo shorts. His legs were tanned and had a fine sprinkling of dark hair covering them. His feet were bare as they slapped against the ground, heading toward us holding a...water pistol.

I didn't have time to register his intent as a wicked grin spread over his face and instead of aiming for the child coming toward us, icy water hit my chest. The feel of the freezing water hitting me with force had the air leaving my lungs in a rush.

"Poppy, Mason got ya," River pointed out in glee as she bounced in her jelly shoes at my side.

It took a second for my lungs to catch up and let me suck in enough breath to answer. "He did," I ground out breathlessly, while I gave Mason a menacing stare that did nothing as he went to take aim again.

I tried to hold up my arm holding the box and use it as a barrier as I growled, "Don't you fuc—"

"Poppy, we's in company," River said sternly as she tugged on the hand she held, distracting me long enough for Mason to hit me with another blast of icy water. Had the stuff come straight from the freezer?

"Fucksake," I hissed as the water that had soaked through my thin T-shirt slid down my chest and into the waistband of my jeans.

Mason laughed as the child stood grinning next to River said, "He said a bad word."

"No shit, kid," I muttered, and continued to glare at Mason, not quite believing he'd had the gall to soak me.

He held his hand up in submission, even as his eyes showed no remorse. "I'm sorry. I don't know what got into me."

"You better hope I don't get you alone or y'all find out what got into you," I muttered under my breath.

When Mason's eyes widened then narrowed on me, I swallowed the sigh for not keeping my thoughts to myself. The light in his eyes was full of challenge and held my gaze. *What the fuck is wrong with me?*

"Ya dripping, Poppy, and soaking my present," River complained as she tugged her hand free from mine.

"Let's take your Poppy inside so he can dry off. Declan, this is not over," Mason declared, waving the water pistol at the kid still standing next to River.

"You'll need to be faster, Uncle Mason, if ya gonna beat me," he stated with childish confidence as he gave everyone a toothy grin.

He looked River up and down and I braced. "I's Declan, I's six. Who's ya?"

"I's River, I's five, and dis is my Poppy," she answered, sounding a little shier than her normal self.

"Hiya River, ya wanna come play with me? De others is all bigger dan me and don't like to play with me, so I's left with Uncle Mason." He shrugged his tiny shoulder, his face full of hope at finding a new friend.

River looked up at me. "Can I's go, Poppy?"

Seeing that there was no way to escape without upsetting River, and refusing to acknowledge the smug smile on Mason's face that said he'd guessed my plan to leave quickly, I nodded, albeit reluctantly. "Just for a little bit, okay?"

She skipped over to Mason, not answering me. "I's made dis for ya." She thrust the colorfully wrapped box at him before she followed Declan up the path. She giggled as Declan whispered something in her ear as they went into the house without a backward glance.

My heart raced as she disappeared.

"She'll be fine. My family aren't monsters that eat children," Mason stated light-heartedly as he walked toward me. The strain I'd noticed the last time we were together was no longer evident as he offered me a relaxed smile.

"I really am sorry about getting you all wet." He slapped a hand over his mouth and started to laugh. "That sounds dirty, right?" he choked out past his laughter. "I take that back. I wouldn't mind getting you wet under the right circumstances." For a second, I couldn't quite believe that he'd said that aloud, and so close to the house his parents lived in.

His face became flushed and the laughter died from his eyes as I struggled to find a response.

"Sorry, you've already pointed out you're not interested."

He went to swing around, and I took hold of his bicep in a firm grip, being careful not to hurt him. "I didn't say I wasn't interested, I said it was a bad idea. It still is, but fuck, I want you. My gut burns with the need to fuck you, fuck you hard into whatever surface is nearest." As I'd already lost my mind and better judgement, I stepped into his body, crowding him.

I lowered my mouth to his ear and mouthed, "You wanna be my bitch?"

Chapter 10

Mason

Thinking my brain had been fried with the heat traveling through me, I sucked in a muggy breath. Had he just asked me to be his bitch?

"Oh, Lincoln, it's so good to see you. Was that River with Declan?" Dad called from behind me, saving me from having to answer Linc.

I kept my lower body twisted away from my Dad, so as not to alert him to the problem I was having. He stood on the porch, his eyes alight with a warm welcome.

"Yeah, that was River," Linc answered, showing no signs of being affected by our conversation.

My Dad eyed Linc's top with some amusement. "You look like you got caught in the battle."

"It appears so." He stiffened at my side, as if he was reminded what we'd been talking about.

"I was just about to bring him inside to see if we could find him a shirt while his dries."

Dad chuckled. "We might have one of Hudson's left in a box somewhere in the guest room. He's the only one that would match Lincoln for size." He waved at Lincoln, "Come on in, and I'll see what I can rustle up for you."

"It's fine, Dad, I'll find something for him." The second the words left my mouth, Lincoln, who'd started to walk toward the house, stopped. His eyes pinned me in place and the silent message he relayed in those few seconds could have melted the blacktop faster than the heat of the Texas sun in a heatwave.

Had I phrased it like that on purpose?

"Fine, make sure you hurry though, the food's just about ready and you know your brothers won't wait." He shifted his gaze to Lincoln. "It's real good to see you and River. I'm glad you could come."

The real sincerity in his voice left me grateful for the man he was. With that, he headed back inside, leaving me with Linc, who looked like he'd been stunned by a taser. All his muscles seemed to be locked in place, then it was as if he suddenly remembered where he was, and his face became an unreadable mask.

My gut twisted into greasy knots at what could possibly happen next as I led him into my family home. Silently, he followed me into the house. His presence dominated all my thoughts as I dropped the water pistol and River's gift down on the hall table. Leading the way up the polished wooden staircase, it creaked and moaned as Linc came up behind me. He was so close behind me, I could feel the heat rolling off his body.

I walked to the end of the long passageway, to the door that had been Hudson's bedroom as a child. Opening the door, I stepped into the room and glanced about. It looked nothing like it had when it had been Hudson's. When he'd lived at home, it had been a complete mess, his clothes strewn about the place, along with magazines, games, and whatever else he could place on the floor.

Now the room resembled a showroom out of one of those fancy magazines my Mom loved. The walls were a muted lemon and the furniture was all white. The large bed that dominated the room was covered in a sunshine yellow cover with massive white daisies on it. There were candles and knickknacks placed precisely apart from each other on pieces of white furniture.

Noise from the party in the back garden carried into the room. I looked back at Linc who remained in the doorway, not entering the room and looking completely out of place.

"I'll see what we've got. If you give me your shirt, I'll put it in the dryer. Shouldn't take but a few minutes to dry it," I rambled, thinking I sounded like an idiot.

I went to the closet, opening the door to search through the couple of boxes marked with Hudson's name on them. Folded at the bottom were a couple of old T-shirts, so I pulled them out and spun around with them clutched in my hand.

All thoughts fled from my mind as Linc stood inside the room, his tanned, hairless chest now bare. My whole body reacted to the visual of firm, rippling muscles. The dips and undulations looked like they'd been air-brushed into his skin. The cum gutters that disappeared into the low-slung jeans were a thing of beauty. A tingling started in my fingertips at thoughts of being able to explore the body in front of me. My gaze drifted back to the two tattoos covering the whole of his upper chest. They were so different, yet equally beautiful.

The calligraphy script with the name 'Lizzie' tattooed over his heart had tendrils coming off the letters and on the ends were tiny flowers in bold colors. The other side of his chest was covered with his club logo.

"Who…" I swallowed past the dryness in my throat as the words got stuck. "Who did the artwork?" I asked, meeting his gaze.

The gold threaded into the brown of his eyes seemed to glow as he cut the distance between us down in just a couple of steps. The tension inside me matched the electrified feel of the air in the room. A dark, sexual energy snapped between us. Unsure who moved first, I found my arms wrapped around Linc's warm, scented, naked upper body.

His mouth claimed mine in a ruthless kiss that left me brutally aroused. His taste flooded my senses as his tongue thrust into my mouth and duelled with mine. He fought for dominance as I fought back, matching his hunger with my own. Teeth clacked together as I got lost in the passion, in Linc, until I couldn't think about anything but him, feel anything but his body pressed against mine.

"Fuck, I don't know why, but I want you," he growled against my mouth, his hands sliding down to my ass and squeezing before he shifted me to grind his dick against mine.

"We...shouldn't...oh fuck." I lost my train of thought as his mouth moved across my jaw to my neck, his teeth raking at the skin, creating tiny flames of desire.

When his teeth sank into my flesh and he bit hard enough to mark me, I had to forcibly think about something else to stop from embarrassing myself and coming in my pants. *This is your parents' home, get a fucking grip. You can't fuck your client.*

My chest heaved as I staggered back and held up my hands to ward him off, only then noticing I still had hold of the T-shirts. They were now a crumpled mess, but there was little I could do about that. I threw them at Linc in defense and they fell to the floor at his feet when he made no move to catch them.

"I...we...this can't happen again." I added as much conviction as I could when Linc's gaze became an impenetrable mask. "I'll take your shirt and meet you downstairs."

He said nothing as he bent and picked up the shirts at his feet. He held out his wet T-shirt, and the coward in me wanted to tell him to bring it down himself, when his gaze challenged me. Instead, I stepped forward and reached out. He didn't immediately hand it over and I sucked in a shaky breath, meeting his gaze head on.

"This isn't over," he growled, then let go of the shirt.

A wild fluttering started in my chest as I took the coward's way out and said nothing. I saw no point in arguing when he'd already felt my arousal against his. I just wasn't ready to face up to what that meant to me, to my job, and to Lincoln.

Instead of going back downstairs after I left Linc to get dressed, I went to the family bathroom. I locked the door behind me, going directly to the double sink and staring in the mirror above. What the fuck had I just done?

Kissed Linc like you'd never kissed another, that's what!

I didn't miss that.

I buried my head in my trembling hands, unable to look at myself a moment longer. My lips were still puffy from Linc's none-too-gentle kiss and his taste lingered in my mouth. I didn't even want to think about the dark, lurid mark I'd noticed on my neck where he'd bitten the skin. The fucker had marked me.

A shudder ran through my body and my dick remained flush against my cargo shorts, aroused and unhappy that I'd stopped. *I thought you weren't going to think about it?*

"I'm not," I muttered as I raised my head and looked myself in the eye. I'd crossed a line, and

I'd never done that before, no matter how tempted I might have been in the past.

It wasn't going to happen again, no matter what Linc said. *Really, you believe that?*

It couldn't, for both our sakes. The stakes were too high, and the price could be his freedom and River. I was coming to realize that I didn't want to jeopardize either. Then why did that leave a hollow feeling in my chest?

Chapter 11

Lincoln

The sound of heavy footfalls came pounding up the stairs, drowning out the buzz of the tattoo gun, followed by Sid bursting into the room. "I'm done with the brothers, you have to come to the club and deal with them," he declared angrily.

The buzz of the gun stopped as I lifted it off the guy lying face down on the bench I used for back tattooing and gave Sid my full attention. His face was flushed with temper and I could all but see steam coming out of his ears. "There's little I can do about it, as you know damn well I can't set foot in the club right now," I spat out, my own temper starting to boil as he glared at me.

Sid's scowl marred his brow and nearly the whole top of his shaven head. His tattooed skull seemed to move, making the serpent tattoo come to life. His face had grease smears on it, as did his hands and clothes, showing he'd come straight from the workshop. "I've had enough of the fucking nitwits, and the pair ain't listening to me. This business is gonna cost us if they keep goin'," he snarled, seemingly unaware the guy on the bench could hear the conversation.

"I can't talk about this now," I said, pointedly looking at the tattoo gun I held and then the guy on the bench, who'd turned his head so he could watch the interaction, as well as listen.

It was the one thing about Sid that pissed me off, he couldn't seem to keep his mouth shut when he was in a foul temper. Mercifully, he didn't lose it often which was why he'd remained my second in command for so long. It did tell me that whatever the brothers had done this time, it must be bad to get Sid to leave the shop and come across town. My stomach dropped and I wanted to curse, the heavy weight attached to my ankle reminding me that I was prevented from dealing with business.

"Fine, I'll be back at closin' if I haven't beaten the shit out of the pair of 'em." With that, he stomped out of the room the same way he'd come in a few moments earlier.

I didn't need him to explain that he was talking about Beau and Ram. The brothers were a fucking nuisance who didn't feel any brotherly love toward each other, and they'd get into it without the slightest provocation.

When they had a joint goal, they managed to keep a lid on their hate for each other. However, that hadn't lasted long when they'd started working in the auto shop. Sid was forever stepping between them and it had been happening more and more recently. Thing was, they were skilled autos who knew their way around most engines. What the fuck was I to do with the pair of them? They'd been members of the club for about seven years. Maybe I should threaten to kick their asses out of the Dark Angels? They'd worked hard to prove their loyalty to me and to their brothers, it just seemed whatever beef they had with each other always overflowed into the shop.

I rubbed my jaw and sighed, setting aside the problem when the guy on the bench started to fidget, drawing my attention back to him. I eyed the half-completed phoenix I'd hand designed coming out of a pile of ash at the base of his back. The outline had been completed on the dude's first visit, then I'd done the ashes across his lower back. They seemed to billow as if caught on the wind, giving a 3D effect.

This was the dude's third appointment, and he'd need another two for me to complete the artwork.

"You good for me to start again?" I asked before laying my gun against his skin.

"Yeah, I'm all good."

Back tattoos could be tricky, especially over more bony areas that could be more painful. I usually did the tricky parts first, so that it got it out of the way once the outline had been completed.

My hair was tied back so it wouldn't get in the way as I bent back over the bench and got back to work, visualising the design and colors as I delicately inked the colorful feathers. By the time the alarm I'd set myself went off to say the dude's time was up, my lower back was aching like a bitch and my fingers were slightly cramping. Those two feelings were signs I'd gotten lost in my work and, as I focused on what I'd done, a small smile tugged at my lips.

Excitement buzzed through me as I pictured the completed tattoo. "I think your gonna piss your pants when you see this."

"Your rep, and the six months I waited, I'll hope for more than pissing my pants," the dude replied as I cleaned his skin and dressed his back. "You will be able to finish it, right? I've heard word you got into a bit of trouble."

He didn't look at me as he carried on talking, and my eyes narrowed. "I'll finish it," I ground out, keeping the questions about what he'd heard to myself.

The silence between us became tense as the dude quickly got up and slipped on his T-shirt.

"Sorry, it's none of my business," he muttered, not meeting my eye.

"Fuckin' right, there," I snarled, then took a deep breath to calm the anger that had fuck all to do with the dude who only wanted to know he'd get his tattoo completed before they tried to throw my ass in jail. "It's cool, I've you booked in for the next two weeks, that should see you done. Check with Nutty before you leave."

He nodded, his face looking a little paler than when he'd come in. "Right, ok, I'll see you next week." With that, he all but ran out the door and I could hear his feet moving rapidly down the stairs.

I twisted my head from side to side and front to back, hoping to release the tight knots across my upper shoulders. When it did little, I gave up and cleaned up my work station and bench, before shifting it to the other side of the room and moving my tattoo chair back into position for the next customer who was getting a half sleeve tattoo on their left arm.

Checking the time I had left, I went to grab a drink, looking to occupy myself so I'd not have any time to think about the shitstorm that was my life right now.

There was the sound of low voices coming from behind Kyle's closed door as I passed, but there was not his usual electric music. Since his return from his trip home, he'd been moody and quiet, two things he wasn't normally. Nutty hadn't been able to weasel out any information from him, which in itself left me worrying something was up. I tended to let Nutty deal with the drama, only this time, I had a feeling it was going to have to be me.

As if I didn't have enough on my plate.

I groaned under my breath as I entered the tiny kitchen and went to the fridge to grab a can of Mountain Dew, switching my thoughts to the one man who was filling my head more than I liked. Mason's absence had been notable since I'd kissed him, and I wasn't sure yet if that was a good or a bad thing. *Good surely, 'cause he can't mess with your head?*

Which head?

I took a deep swallow from the now open can, to get rid of the dryness in my mouth at recalling the aching arousal he'd left me with. It hadn't abated as I'd stood watching him move from group to group, avoiding me for most of the time I'd stayed at his parents' home.

Surprisingly, I'd ended up staying for the whole afternoon. Any misgivings I'd had that the folks would run a mile from me and River had been proven wrong. Yeah, there had been a couple of raised eyebrows, but with Mr. Davenport and his whole family being real hospitable, others had followed their example. They'd included me and River as if we'd been long-time friends.

Truthfully, it had weirded me out a little. River, on the other hand, had been in her element. With Declan following her everywhere, she'd gone from shy to full-on chatterbox. The memory of her sitting next to Mason while he'd opened the gift she'd made for him, floated to the surface of my mind.

"Dids ya open up my gift Mason?" River's voice carried to me as I stood nursing the one beer I'd allow myself when I was driving. I'd stood in the shade of the porch, feeling a little uncomfortable after the ribbing I'd gotten for wearing Hudson's T-shirt, that was a little too tight.

Mason's expression turned sheepish and he shook his head. "I was waiting to do it with you." River didn't notice the obvious lie, but I did. Mason glanced up and caught me staring at him. The T-

shirt he wore had been pulled up to cover the mark I'd made on his neck, and for a second, I wanted to go and pull the material away so everyone could see he was mine.

Get a fucking grip!

"I'll go grab it, gimme a sec." Mason bounded up the back-porch steps and disappeared into the house behind me. River came toward me, her arms open for me to lift her up. I placed her onto my hip and nuzzled her neck, making her laugh.

"Poppy, ya's tickling me with ya whiskers." Her giggles increased as I kept going.

At the sound of the porch door slamming shut, River moved her head back.

"Mason, save me from Poppy's whiskers," she cried, her arms reaching for Mason.

My heart skipped a beat when Mason didn't hesitate and whisked my little girl out of my arms, stating in a stage whisper, "I'll save you from the whiskery monster."

Her laughter continued as she clung to his neck, her eyes alight with joy as she looked back at me and rested her head on Mason's shoulder.

Fuck! Look at them.

My fingers tightened on the beer bottle as Mason kissed her head without a thought and gave me a wide grin that I felt all the way down to my toes. Not quite convinced I wasn't looking as dopey as Mason, I made sure to keep the smile off my face.

There was a flash of disappointment on Mason's face, but it was quickly masked as he sat on the porch step, placing the small box he held on the floor before he settled River in his lap. Then he picked the box back up, making cooing noises over the childish wrapping. He carefully removed the tape to reveal the box she'd decorated with gemstones, glitter, and other sparkly bits she loved to collect and use.

The lid had his name written in glitter pen, though given I could actually read it, I was pretty sure Nutty had helped out with that part. River looked expectantly at Mason as he stared at the box, his eyes misting with tears.

The second he looked at River, I saw real emotion in the depths of his eyes. "It's beautiful, and I have several special keepsakes I'm gonna put in it when I go home. I'm going to put this in a special place so folks can see it when they come to my home."

River beamed at him, then at me. "Dat's nice, and just like my Poppy. He puts all my presents wheres folks can see em."

I blamed the afternoon Texas sun for the flush of heat that rose up my face when Mason grinned at me.

The wild beating of my heart against my ribs pulled me up short, and I took a deep swig from the chilled drink I held. *Think about something else, anything.*

My mind cast about for something, anything, that would distract me from the weird emotions coursing through me as I recalled the tender moment.

I ran a hand over the top of my head, dislodging the band holding my hair back, reminding me of Nola's attempt to run her hands through my hair. A shudder of disgust ran through me.

The bitch had been ramping things up with her lies, which were getting more and more outrageous with each telling. It seemed she wanted to cause a spectacle, that was for sure. If that wasn't bad enough, she'd attempted to become a prospect at the club while I was blocked by the judge from the place. The stupid fucker had petitioned those in the inner circle that cast votes.

Sid and Davey had alerted me, but the four other members that made up the seven man vote with mine, Ricky, Stevie, Ned, and Doddie, hadn't thought to mention it. I'd been messaging them, but the lack of response, though not uncommon in the older members, was still odd after I'd been incarcerated.

I leaned back against the counter and stared unseeingly at the wall in front of me covered with River's artwork. Was someone trying to set me up? The feeling in my gut said something was wrong. And it was increasing daily with Mason sending me messages, complaining about the stonewalling the members were doing. In particular, he'd mentioned Ricky, Stevie, and Ned, the old timers that had been a part of the club for as far back as I could remember. They'd all been loyal to Swifty. Had they been working behind my back to oust me and take over Dark Angels?

The club and the businesses were all connected. That meant income generated from my two businesses supported the clubhouse and members who needed extra cash. I'd brought the club into the twenty-first century with the new building and working on removing the criminal element that had been an established part of club life.

My Granddaddy had used the auto shop as a chop shop for stolen parts, taking high-end stolen cars and breaking them down for parts and selling them on. Back in his day, it had been easier than it was today with all the new technology for tracking cars and car parts. There'd been the side-line in stolen electronics, too, and a few other things that the guys could get their hands on.

Again, River had changed the way I viewed things, and although I'd had some battles, the profits from both the legit auto shop and River's Tattoo more than made up for lost income.

"Linc, your next customer is here," Nutty shouted from the bottom of the stairs.

I threw the now empty bottle into the bin as I passed it, and headed back to my room, pushing aside the worry for now. There'd be plenty of time for that later, when Sid came back.

I swallowed a sigh, concentrating on clearing my head for my next client.

Chapter 12

Mason

I sat opposite Ned and jotted down what he said, not that he offered up much. "So, you left at one am and Nola was still in the clubhouse." I'd come back for a third time to see if I could gain any more insight into what had happened between Nola and Linc. I wasn't satisfied with what I'd found so far, and the court date had already been set for the following month.

Nola's lawyer was applying a lot of pressure to get things moving and, with the sheriff's office more than willing to go along with it, I was starting to feel the strain with so little evidence to support Linc's testimony that nothing had happened. There had been evidence that Nola had endured rough sex that night, but there'd been no DNA found in the swabs that had been taken, so, at the moment, it was his word against hers.

"Yep. I told you that about ten fuckin' times, how many more times do you need me to say it?" he spat out, his face wearing a scowl as his cheeks flushed. Sweat beaded on his forehead as he looked anywhere but at me.

The air conditioning in the clubhouse whirred in the background and made me suspicious as to why Ned was sweating like a pig about to be spit roasted. My eyes narrowed on him, and I continued to push at him when something felt off. "Who was present in the clubhouse that night? Can you run me through everyone who was here?"

He rolled his bloodshot eyes that spoke to how much he liked to drink, as did the stale smell of liquor coming off him as he continued to sweat in the cool room. As he recited the list of names, something struck me that I'd previously missed. I waited till he was finished before asking, "Wasn't Nutty here?" I wasn't sure why I'd not noticed her absence before. Had she been with River?

"Nah, Nutty had a date with a guy from your neck of the woods, a bloke from Killeen. We're not good enough for Miss High 'n' Mighty," he ground out, his eyes going mean.

I struggled to keep my face blank at the thought of this guy with someone as nice as Nutty. I couldn't place Ned's age, but he looked like he'd around been around the block a few times. His sparse hair, jowly jaw, and beer gut that hung over the jeans he wore weren't something that said, 'pick me as a partner.'

"So Nutty wasn't looking after River that night?" The second I asked the question, something akin to fear passed over Ned's face before he could mask it.

"Who knows where River was. Killer could 'ave left her with anyone." The way he said it made it sound like Linc left River with any random person, as if he didn't care about who looked after her.

A spark of temper sizzled to life at the obvious lie, and I had to work to keep my expression neutral.

Why would Ned act like that when he'd been a member of the club for decades and knew Linc better than some? The question lingered as I swallowed the bitterness gathering in my throat. Was I missing something? If so, what was it?

I finished off pretty soon after, letting Ned amble off to the busy bar tucked into the far corner of the massive room. The first time I'd driven out to the clubhouse I'd been surprised by the sheer size and expanse of the building. The place looked like a luxury cabin rather than a biker clubhouse. Inside there were polished wood walls and floors that were well maintained. There were black, leather sofas scattered about the main room, and dark grey rugs on the floor. There was a massive fireplace and above it the club logo was handcrafted into the wood.

The bar in the far corner was made of the same wood as the cabin and blended with the room. The several times I'd been there, there was always someone manning it for the men and few women scattered about the room. Men and women alike wore a patch showing evidence of their allegiance to the club. The ones with no patch, I'd been informed, were prospects looking to become a member. It seemed that had been Nola's intention, only she hadn't wanted to go through the same process as others to prove she was worth a patch. Not that Sid had explained what that entailed as he'd walked me through the building.

He'd been a little more forthcoming than some of the other men as he'd shown me the pool room and several bedrooms, all with their own facilities. There was a meeting room they called the church, I assumed because it was only used for private business. Linc had his own personal space in the back, which explained why no one had seen or allegedly heard anything that night.

Linc had said that Nola had followed him into his private rooms. Nola, on the other hand, said he'd been all over her and invited her in. Not quite the picture I was getting, but it seemed she'd been around him most of the night, if I were to believe what people were telling me. And that she'd left at the same time as him. Ned had more than implied that Linc liked to fuck, and often, and that he wasn't particularly fussy. Again, it didn't gel with the man whose biggest concern was the child he'd been left to care for on his own.

My gaze swept the room, and I noted the unguarded, hate-filled eyes watching me. How could Linc create a cabin as beautiful as the land it was sitting on, and not notice something was horribly wrong here? A shiver raced down my spine at thoughts of why the club might have been set deep in the woods, not far from Nolan Creek. The place offered isolation and a freedom for the men to do as they pleased.

The Dark Angels were well known around these parts. When I'd gone digging in the news archives, I'd gained a picture of the men and the activities the club had been involved in. Something had changed around the time River had been born. There were hardly any mentions about the club and only a few altercations with the law for minor stuff. Had they gotten better at hiding the illegal practices?

The businesses seemed to be above board, but the cash Linc had at his disposal was questionable. My gut twisted at what that possibly meant.

I'd set my worries aside about where the cash came from, or I'd tried to, so that I could keep a clear head and focus on Linc's case. The last thing I wanted was to rock any other gremlins free that I didn't want or need.

I leaned back against the leather seat and ignored the tension in the room as I thought about what I needed to do next. Up till now, I'd avoided going to River's Tattoo. If I'd needed to talk to Linc, I'd either sent a message or called him. It seemed I was going to have to go and talk to Nutty, because I had a hunch about what Linc had done with River the night Nola said she was attacked, and I needed to see if I was right.

The number of cars and motorcycles parked on the drive at River's meant I had to park further down the street. I eyed the clear blue sky and wondered why I longed for summer, but the moment the temperature started to climb, I wanted it to be fall?

I removed my suit jacket and slung it over the car seat before rolling up my shirt sleeves. Reaching for my briefcase, I got out of the car. The midday heat had my shirt sticking uncomfortably to my skin as I walked along the sidewalk back to Linc's shop.

Again, I found it at odds with the man Linc presented to the world that he'd chosen a quiet, suburban neighborhood for his home and business. I strolled up the path and walked into the shop.

The reception room had been converted into a waiting area and split in two. The left side had several comfy seats that were all taken. There was a table with magazines, and a mini fridge with a glass front housing several different drinks for customers to take.

On the right-hand side of the room, Nutty stood behind a large, handcrafted desk that looked more like a bar. The wood went all the way to the floor and hid most of Nutty behind it.

She beamed at me and mouthed "Hang on," then carried on talking into the phone she held to her ear while she wrote something in the large book open in front of her. Her inky black hair was in its usual spiky style, but she wore no make-up today. Her tanned skin glowed with health and her silvery eyes twinkled with humor as she continued to chat with whoever was on the other end of the phone.

My gaze swept the room and registered the people waiting for their appointments. There was an eclectic mix, from leather clad bikers, to a guy in a three-piece suit, and a girl who didn't look old enough to be making decisions about inking her body.

"What can I do for you Mason? If you're after Linc, your gonna have a bit of a wait, he's got a customer up in his room."

"Actually, it's you I came to see." I gave her a reassuring smile when hers dimmed and she started to fidget with the pen she'd been using.

"Why?"

"Listen, can you give me a few minutes, somewhere private," I glanced back at the full chairs then back at Nutty. "Please."

Her smooth brow furrowed, and she chewed at her lower lip. "Gimme a minute, I'll see if someone can cover the desk for me." She sounded reluctant, but I nodded and leaned against the desk as she wandered off down a hall, disappearing into a room.

My fingers drifted up to the side of my throat without thought, and I touched the shirt that covered the now faded mark. Any doubts I might have had that Linc was bi or gay had fled the second he'd laid his mouth on mine. It had also created more questions about why no one at the club had, at any point, mentioned Linc being gay, or at least, bi.

Did he hide it? I shook my head. His 'fuck you' attitude didn't vibe with him hiding his sexuality. Yet, not once had anyone brought it up. Why was that? Were they protecting Linc? Or was there some other reason?

A throbbing started in my temples by the time Nutty reappeared with a guy that I'd not met. He had a mop of blond hair and a sunny smile. He stood around the same height as me, but he was super skinny and something about him told me he might be gay.

When his aqua blue eyes roamed over my body in appreciation, my suspicions were confirmed.

"Who's this?" the guy asked, his eyes alight with amusement.

Nutty rolled her eyes, but I didn't fail to notice how she stiffened. "This is Mason Davenport, Linc's lawyer. And the reason I need a couple minutes of your time, Troy." She kept her voice low so the folks sat in the chairs couldn't hear. Her voice was cheery, yet I wasn't getting the impression she was feeling it.

I held out my hand and got a firm handshake in return. "Nice to meet you, Troy. I hopefully won't keep Nutty too long."

After dropping my hand, he waved off my worry. "It's cool," he glanced at the seated area, "Wendy won't mind waiting, will you, love?" he asked in a raised voice to attract her attention from the magazine she held.

The girl who didn't look old enough, nodded and blushed a deep shade of red.

"Come on, let's go up to the apartment," Nutty stated.

I followed her as she led the way up the couple flights of stairs to Linc's apartment. The first evening I'd come up, I'd found a home that was both comfortable and showed River's influence everywhere. The amount of pink was a little overwhelming, but totally adorable.

Nutty led us into the large lounge area that had windows that overlooked the big back garden. The garden had a huge fence around it so no one could see in. There was a fire pit and a large barbecuing area.

The back porch, that must have been added to the second floor, was beneath the window and had the same rainbow table and chairs as was on the main porch, which said that Linc's room was directly beneath.

"So, what is it you wanna ask?"

Chapter 13

Lincoln

My throbbing headache had started about the same time I'd gone downstairs and found Troy manning the reception desk. What did Mason want with Nutty?

The same question was on repeat in my head as I finished cleaning the client's skin.

"You do spectacular work. I can't wait to figure out where I'll have my next tat," the guy all but gushed as he eyed his left arm. It might have been red and bleeding, but it didn't detract from the art.

The intertwining flowers were in bold shades of blue and green. I'd blended the colors and faded them out toward the end of the petals. The stamen were bright yellow on thin green stalks. The flowers went around the whole upper arm and were threaded with thorns that looked as if they'd dug into his flesh, with several drops of blood seeming to drip down his forearm toward the back of his hand. I'd worked with the guy on the design, and I'd been stoked with how it had turned out.

"Maybe you need to do the other arm," I suggested as I eyed the bare arm, my creative mind already considering the options.

"I'm thinkin' my right leg," he muttered thoughtfully.

"Cool." I started reeling off the instructions on how to care for the tattoo and eventually had to push him out the door. He was still on the high from getting his tattoo completed and could have talked for hours.

Cleaning down my workstation, I rolled my neck back and forth. When my hand started to cramp, I rubbed at my fingers, trying to loosen the tightness. Nutty's dark head appeared around the door, looking visibly upset, but she didn't get a chance to say anything before Mason stepped around her.

One look at his angry face, and it didn't take a rocket scientist to figure out I'd been caught holding out on him.

"Why didn't you tell me River was with you the night Nola says you raped her?"

His blunt question had Nutty's head disappearing, and I felt the throbbing at my temples increase.

"It's got nothin' to do with what happened—"

He stepped so close to me I could feel his breath touch my face as he spat out angrily, "I'll be the judge of whether it's got anything to do with what happened. I told you that I need honesty. How the fuck am I supposed to trust you when you're holding stuff back from me?"

My own temper started to rise at being called out. I stood taller, making every inch count as I towered over him, making him have to lift his chin to keep eye contact. "I'll be the judge of what's important, not you."

His face became an impenetrable mask, but not before what looked like hurt flashed into his eyes. He ran a hand through his hair as he stared at me, then spoke in an icy tone that chilled me to the bone.

"Is that right? Well you tell me then how the fuck I'm gonna stop your ass from being thrown into jail for the next God-knows-how-long for rape. Because the way the fucking club members are stonewalling and Nola is gathering support, you'll be lucky to see the outside of a cell for a very long time. When you think you're ready to be honest, you know where to find me."

Far calmer than I expected, he spun on his heel and stalked out of the room. His back was rigid, and his feet thudded solidly against the wooden stairs as he disappeared from sight.

"Well, fuck!"

"Poppy, what did ya do?" River asked as she came into the room, her face full of worry. "Why was Mason angry at ya, Poppy? I could 'ear him as I was comin' downstairs. Will he come back to help us?" Her voice was full of tears and matched the now shiny eyes peering up at me, striking at the anger and leaving me cold with dread that I'd fucked up.

Crouching down in front of her, I opened my arms for her. The second it took for her to decide to come to me showed how much I'd fucked up. "I'm sorry, Spirit. I'll fix it with Mason." I buried my nose in her scented hair and inhaled.

"Now Poppy! Ya need to fix it now." Her tone brooked no further argument and I sighed, knowing I'd do anything to remove the sadness from her face.

"Okay. Wanna come with me?" I knew it was the coward's thing to do, but I needed Mason to see that I couldn't use River and put her through an ordeal that no child should endure. I'd suffered as a child through neglect, careless adults, and both physical and verbal abuse. That was not the life I wanted for River. So why couldn't Mason see that?

You never told him your reasons, so how would he know?

Silently cursing the voice of reason, I held on to River as I rose. I dug my wallet out of my back pocket to search for the card Mason had given me with his contact details on it. He'd handwritten his address on the back, saying it was for emergencies only. This was an emergency of sorts, wasn't it?

I went in search of Nutty. Half an hour later, after she'd apologized like forty times and I'd explained I wasn't mad at her, I left with River. Riding my hog, she clung on to her special made belt as I rode highway 35 to Killeen after figuring out where Mason's apartment block was.

All too soon, we were stood outside his apartment door with a box of cakes from a bakery just down the street that River had spotted and insisted we buy Mason a treat to say sorry.

"Poppy, stop scowlin', yous'll frighten Mason lookin' like dat," she scolded.

My teeth gritted together as I worked on trying to relax my face, the headache making it hard to focus. Before I could knock on the door,

River was using the side of her tiny fist to bang on the door.

Silent minutes ticked by, and I considered if I should maybe have rung to check he was home, but then River banged again.

The thought fled when Mason opened the door wearing nothing but a large cream towel wrapped around his lean hips. Droplets of water clung to his hair and muscular chest as he stood there, his eyes widening. Then the unreadable mask was back in place while I struggled to unglue my tongue from the roof of my mouth.

"Yes?"

"Now don't be mean to Poppy, he came to says sorry to ya. Ya have to listen 'cause it's polite. Well dat's what Nutty says," River explained as she let go of my hand and sailed past Mason into his apartment, without asking if she could come in.

The squeal of delight she released was followed by Mason spinning around to give me the sight of his broad back and the two dimples at the base of his spine. The tug of arousal I felt whenever he was near ramped up, and my jeans became far snugger than they'd been on the ride over. With his back to me, I adjusted myself and followed him into the apartment as he walked over to where River stood.

I shut the door behind me, and then looked to see what had caught River's attention. My heart rolled in my chest at the sight of the little box she'd made. It sat on top of a tall cabinet in an alcove next to a huge flat screen TV, mounted in front of a large muted grey sofa. *He'd done as he'd said!*

"Look, Poppy, Mason putted my box right where folks can see," she said with such happiness that I couldn't swallow for a second.

"He did." It was the best I could come up with when Mason turned his thoughtful, sea-green eyes on me.

He moved his gaze to River, then back to me, before closing the distance between us. He shook his head. "That's a dirty trick to pull on me when you know I'm mad at you," he muttered, low enough for me to hear but not River.

I didn't pretend not to understand and gave him a stoic look.

He sighed. "What are you doing here?" he asked, then his nose twitched before he sniffed the air, releasing a low groan as he eyed the bakery box I held. "Is that from Myla's bakery?" He rubbed at his naked stomach and drew my attention to the firm, tanned skin.

"Was my idea, wasn't it, Poppy?" River interjected, breaking the tension between us.

"Go get dressed, then we can talk," I rasped through a parched throat, his fingers running over his damp skin as if he were teasing me.

For a moment, I thought he was going to argue, but when he walked off toward one of the four doors leading off the living room, I released the pent-up breath I'd held.

I scratched at my head. Why did I think this was a good idea again?

I blew out a breath. Whether it was a good idea or not, I had little choice if I wanted to keep River safe. I just needed to keep reminding myself this was about River, and nothing more.

Chapter 14

Mason

I took my time getting dressed, needing a few minutes to get myself under control. There's a child out there, and with Linc looking hotter than a runway model, that's what I needed to remember.

My cheeks puffed out and I rolled my eyes in the mirror as I combed my hair and eyed the loose-fitting shorts and T-shirt I'd put on. Should I get changed into something a little more professional? *It's your home for pity's sake.*

Before I could change my mind, I walked out of the room barefooted, moving silently over the wooden laminate floor. I stood in the doorway and watched River stare up at the box she'd made me. Her face continued to hold the wonder that she'd shown when she'd first seen it sitting in a place of honor on my cabinet.

Linc sat on the edge of my couch, wearing his traditional black jeans and T-shirt, looking very uncomfortable and making me wonder if River had somehow talked him into coming here.

"Have you two had something to eat?" I asked as I stepped fully into the room, my home feeling somewhat smaller with Linc in it. They both turned to look at me, but it was River I focused on.

"We's came straight 'ere so Poppy didn't have a chance to make me supper," River announced, drawing a curse from Linc.

"Then let's see what I have to eat, as I'm so starved, I might just eat whatever is in that box your Poppy brought before my meal." I winked at her and she giggled, coming toward me and offering her arms up for me to pick her up.

I automatically stooped to lift her up without thinking about it, so used to doing it with Hudson's boy, Declan, that it took a moment to register Linc's stillness. Over River's head, I met his stare and raised a brow in question.

His dark eyes held mine. "Can you cook?" he asked.

I suspected that had not been what was on his mind, but I shrugged and answered, "You're about to find out."

"Poppy's a good cook, aren't ya, Poppy?" River glanced to Linc and gave him a sunny smile, then started to chatter about her day as I strolled into the kitchen, not waiting for Linc to follow. I perched River on one of the stools next to the breakfast bar and went to the fridge.

Upon inspection, I found a homemade lasagne my Mom had given to my Dad for me the day before. It was big enough to feed three. "Do we like lasagne? It's my Mom's speciality, I'll bet you've never tasted anything better," I bragged, as I took it out of the fridge and laid it on the counter, doing my best to not look at the silent man leaning against the counter just inside the kitchen doorway.

When I got two yeses, I offered Linc a seat as I moved about the kitchen, feeling more and more self-conscious as I felt two sets of eyes watching my every move. River became silent, and I wondered if she felt the tension between me and Linc.

When the lasagne was in the microwave oven, I set the table and found myself searching for something to say. In the five minutes it took to heat the food, the kitchen smelled like an Italian restaurant and the shower I'd taken to cool off seemed wasted when I was sweating my ass off.

It was a relief to sit down and eat, once I'd offered drinks and plated up food for everyone.

"Thanks Mason, dis smells lovely." River sniffed above her plate then gave Linc a hard stare.

I bit the inside of my cheek to keep the smile from spreading over my face when Linc grudgingly thanked me for dinner.

We ate in silence until we were disturbed by the sound of a mobile phone ringing. Knowing from the ringtone that it wasn't mine, I figured it had to be Linc's. He placed his fork down before tilting his hip to reach into his pocket. His face became pinched as he looked at the screen before he answered. Before he could say a word, the sound of an irritated voice came through the speaker. Though it wasn't loud enough to hear what was being said, the tone was unmistakably angry.

River carried on eating, acting as if this was nothing new to her, so I followed her lead.

"I'm sorry, something came up," Linc muttered. A stain of deep red spread across his cheekbones and his gaze roamed the room behind me.

He muttered several "yep" and "no" answers, but little else as his expression became a mask of fury. He finished the call with an "I'll see you in an hour," before hanging up with no goodbye.

"Something wrong?" The question was out before I could consider it was none of my business, especially after earlier.

His gaze went straight to River, who was now watching him with big sorrowful eyes. "What is it, Poppy?"

"Spirit, I need to talk with Mason alone—"

"No Poppy, dat's not how it works," she interrupted, her face utterly serious, belying her young age. "We's always got to be honest with each other, you's say so."

Linc cursed and got up off the chair that had been facing River to come around and crouch next to her. Something I noticed he did when he spoke to her, so they were on the same level. It was so endearing, I missed the beginning of what he was saying.

"—different, Spirit, the things I need to talk about are for adults and not things for a little girl to hear."

Her brow crumpled and her eyes sheened. Her chin wobbled as she spoke with anger. "I call bullshit, Poppy."

My fork clattered to my plate as my eyes widened in disbelief. Had she just said bullshit? I eyed the pair of them, who seemed oblivious to me. The stern look on Linc's face said I'd heard right.

"Now you listen here, missy, that's no language for a little girl," he chastised in a stern, fatherly voice my own dad would have been proud of.

She rolled her eyes, and for the life of me, I couldn't stop the tickle of amusement that made it impossible to keep a straight face. I glanced away, struggling to watch the interaction and not laugh out loud.

"Poppy, you's use bad language all da time. I know all the words." Her mouth opened as if she were about to recite them and Linc laid a finger on her lips and shook his head. They stared at each for a long time, as if having some silent communication, before Linc got up, lifted her off the seat, and sat in the chair next to me with River on his lap.

"There's a bit of trouble at the auto shop I need to deal with, so we need to get this over with quick," Linc stated in a voice that sounded anything but happy. His gaze held mine and I instantly got that River had won. That as much as he hated what was coming, he'd keep his promises to a little girl who clearly meant more to him than anything else.

If I'd thought before that I'd found him attractive, this took it to a whole new level, and

I had to steel against the emotions that wanted to remove my common sense.

"I held back information, but I had good reasons." Linc's eyes dropped to the top of River's head before meeting mine.

Although he didn't say sorry, it was there in the depths of his eyes, and realizing how hard that probably was for him, I nodded so he understood that I'd gotten his silent apology. When his shoulders visibly relaxed, I exhaled shakily.

How was I going to play this?

"Was River with you the night Nola came to the clubhouse?" I was careful to phrase it so that River wouldn't pick up on what I was really asking.

Before Linc could answer, River spoke. "Nola wants to be Poppy's girlfriend. Ned told her that Poppy would like dat."

I'm sure my expression mimicked Linc's look of disbelief as River carried on.

"Poppy likes boys, not girls, isn't that right, Poppy?" She stated it so matter of fact, I was left in no doubt that he'd spoken to her about his sexual orientation. She didn't wait for a reply but carried on. "Nola was shouting at Poppy and woke me up when we's was at the clubhouse. Poppy told Nola to...well he said a bad word and she shouted then slammed the door. I's quickly got back into bed and Poppy came in and curled up on the sofa next to my bed. He likes to keep me safe, don't ya, Poppy?" She beamed at Linc and I grinned at her.

The second Linc met my gaze, I knew I had a battle on my hands. There was mortification, anger, and something I couldn't interpret, but I had a plan that might overcome whatever his issues were.

"Whatever your thinkin', no. Spirit is not getting dragged into this."

I held up my hand in a peace offering. "What if I can get the judge to meet with River behind closed doors so she can repeat what she saw? Her testimony could get the case thrown out of court, Linc. They have no case with this testimony."

I could feel the excitement at what this meant, then I saw Linc's closed expression. "I get your concern, but this could make all the difference," I begged. "At least give it some thought."

River glanced between the two of us and I could see her trying to figure out what was going on. "Poppy, I's help. Like you's help me all da time." Her earnest expression melted my heart and Linc gave me a threatening scowl.

"I'll think about it." I ignored the lack of enthusiasm and took it as a win that he'd at least agreed to think about what I'd said.

Not long after that, they left, the bakery box left on the side remaining unopened. As I cleaned up the kitchen, I felt a spark of hope that we had a chance to get the charges dropped. Then my life could get back to the way it was before Linc blew in and knocked me on my ass.

What, boring? Empty? All work, with no one to ignite a spark of desire? Yeah, that sounds much better.

I suppose, if put like that, it didn't sound so great.

He's a client.

Not if you get the charges dropped, he won't be.

JP Sayle

Chapter 15

Lincoln

I sat on the couch and stared into my half empty glass of Jack and listened to Sid, dread curling in the pit of my stomach.

The bastards had been working against me! My suspicion that something was off was now confirmed, but it gave me no satisfaction that I'd been right. How had I fucking missed that four of my inner circle were back stabbing scum fuckers?

Anger boiled beneath the surface of my skin, heating my whole body as Sid kicked me in the balls with the truth.

"I ain't said anything about my suspicions, 'cause I wanted to be sure, but when Ram lost it today and punched Beau's lights out, it all came out. Ram overheard Beau talkin' to Ned about how, with you in jail, they could go back to the ol' ways." Sid cracked his knuckles, a habit he had when he was building up a head of steam.

Sid gave a humorless laugh. "The fuckin' ole timers don't know shit. The club has prospered, and the number of prospects has more than tripled. People wanna be a part of the club because it offers a chance for more than kickin' the shit outta someone. Not that that ain't fun and still on the agenda for stupid idiots. And though I'll admit I wasn't sure of the new direction you wanted to take with legalizin' everythin', the auto shop has really taken off.

"You more than proved that, without the heat of the deputies breathin' down our necks, and by workin' hard on business opportunities, we've more than doubled our income. The couple of new prospects we've taken on to do custom paint work. Fuck man, they could compete with your artwork, I swear." His anger faded a little as he mentioned the two men that he'd been eager to try out to bring in new business.

What he'd said about his misgivings about the changes I'd made were nothing new, he'd voiced them all when I'd decided to change things up. For the six months after Lizzie's death, Sid had shouldered the burden of the club while I'd gone to battle with the hospital and the courts to keep River. It had been a bad time and I'd been in a dark place. When I'd won those battles, I'd stood and sworn over Lizzie's gravestone that I'd keep River safe. The changes I'd seen as essential had caused a few rumblings, but as president, I'd made them anyway. Had those changes dug me a grave by my own crew?

It looked like they had!

Would I change them? *Fuck, no.*

Then what was I going to do about the traitors?

I took a sip of Jack and let the alcohol sit in my mouth for a few seconds to burn away the bitter taste of betrayal.

I'd had no time to think about what Mason had suggested, as by the time I'd gotten home and settled River in bed, Sid had been waiting. With everything that had happened with Mason earlier, I'd forgotten Sid was coming back to talk to me. He'd been none too pleased to find I wasn't home, hence the angry call I'd had at Mason's.

When Sid picked up his drink and downed it in one swallow, my eyes narrowed on him and, for the first time that night, I considered that maybe Mason's plan would solve one issue and leave me free to deal with cleaning up the shit at the club. "I think we've a little house cleaning to do," I ground out through clenched teeth.

I sat forward when Sid shifted closer to me.

"Let's hear what you got in mind." His grin was pure evil and reminded me of why he was my second in command.

🐾 🐾 🐾

"Spirit, get a wiggle on, Mina's here," I called down the hallway as Mina gave me a bubbly smile.

She'd been the welcoming committee to the neighborhood four and a half years ago, and though I'd been a little 'get the fuck out of my face', she'd persevered.

Her hubby, Joe, often referred to her as a pit bull, and once she clamped her jaws, she was not letting go. It was a good description, other than it not matching the bubbly personality and petite body that was only five-foot-tall in barefeet. Her dimpled cheeks and sunny blonde hair hid a spine of steel and a will that couldn't be broken. The woman was not someone to mess with, which was why I'd come to trust her with River.

"Hey, sweetie pie, you need anything in town? I'm planning to go shopping 'cause Joe is off for a few days fixing the back porch...*again*," she rolled her big eyes at me.

Joe was an accountant for one of the local firms in town and if I believed Mina, was about as useful as a hand wrench to tattooing. He made enough money to allow her to stay home and take care of the brood, but when it came to the extras, they struggled. Joe then took it upon himself to try and fix the things that were broken, only he seemed to spend more time fixing the repairs he'd made.

"Matt Carstair, one of the guys from the club, has a carpentry business. I could get you a discount." I calculated how to work it so I could shoulder most of the cost without making it obvious. Mina took no money for looking after River. I paid in tats, but she put herself out for me and River all the time, and I hated to be indebted to anyone.

She waved me off as River came bounding down the hall, her hair all over the place. "What have you done to your hair? It looks like a bird's nest."

River giggled and tugged on a few strands and squinted to see what Mina was talking about. "I's not sure. Poppy, can's ya help me?"

Mina winked at me, "I'll do it when we get to my house. Luna is waitin' in the car for you." She took hold of River's hand and glanced back at me. "Did you need any shoppin'?"

With the few things I needed added to her list, Mina left as quickly as she arrived, leaving me time to think about the call I was about to make to Mason. I'd talked everything over with Sid last night and he'd agreed with Mason that this could get rid of at least half of my problems.

After he'd left, I'd then sat down with Nutty, the only other person I trusted to give me solid advice when it came to River. She'd been a little more concerned than Sid about what it all meant for River, and she'd given me some questions I needed answered before I put River onto any kind of firing line.

Picking up my phone, I dug out my wallet and dialed Mason's personal number, hoping to catch him before he went to work. The phone rang several times before it went to voicemail.

"Fuck!" I exclaimed, then realized I was talking to the message service. "Call me when you get this message." With that, I hung up and slipped my wallet back into my pocket. I took the phone with me as I headed down into my work room and laid it on the counter that held my tattoo guns, inks, gloves, needle boxes, and design pads and pens.

"Yo, your down early this mornin'," Kyle mused from the open doorway.

I shrugged. I didn't have a fixed time that I came down after River was set for the day. When I met his stare, the sense something had happened when he'd gone home, returned. My brows rose as I noticed what he was wearing. His usual attire of scruffy jeans and ripped band T-shirt had been replaced with a button-down shirt and Levis that looked like they were brand new.

"You goin' somewhere classy?"

He stiffened and kicked at the wooden floor with the toe of his polished boot. "Nah, I'm just makin' more of an effort, is all."

"Then why do you look like a dude whose being led up the aisle by a gun-tottin'-Daddy?" I evidently failed to keep my humor in check when he glowered, swung about, and stomped off. "Fuck man, I was only jokin'," I shouted after him, only to be met with a blast of music that made the wall throb.

My phone chose to ring then, and I swore as I picked it up and had to shout into it to be heard over the music. "Gimme a sec."

I headed back up to the apartment and shut the door, blocking most of the hideous sound that, as far as I was concerned, could not be called music.

"You upset someone?" Mason asked in a husky voice that gave me tiny goosebumps.

"Somethin' like that," I muttered as I strolled away from the door toward the large window overlooking the back garden. "I need to talk to you."

"Okay, I've back to back appointments all day. I can come over tonight, if that works?" he offered, sounding a little cautious.

"That works… You wanna have supper with me an' River?" I cursed the uncertainty in my voice when I heard his sharp, indrawn breath.

There was a moment of silence before he answered. "Yeah, I'd like that. I'll bring dessert as you never got any last night."

Was he talkin' about himself or real dessert?

"Right…ok…River will be home at six." Heat rode up my face at the stuttering. What was fucking wrong with me, acting all weird and shit?

"I'll be there about then, maybe a little later, but I'll make sure I'm not too late."

His voice held a wealth of amusement as I ended the call. I stared out the window, seeing nothing but thoughtful sea-green eyes that seemed to have hooked themselves into me whether I wanted them there or not.

Last thing I could afford was to get mixed up with him. His life was nothing like mine and I needed to remember that. His family had given him a loving, stable life. Mine had left me to the wolves without a thought.

I rubbed at Lizzie's tattoo. I'd been broken once before, and it had taken River to pull me back from the edge. Something told me that if Mason sunk his hooks into me any deeper, I might well be left with fatal wounds to my heart when he decided to unhook himself from the likes of me.

The hollowness that followed, left me cold as I swung away from the blurring window and went to go lose myself in something that would make me forget, if only for a short while, what I had no place wanting.

JP Sayle

Chapter 16

Mason

The day had been never-ending and as I got into my car, the last thing I wanted to do was drive anywhere but home. A cool shower followed by a beer was what I wanted, but instead, I drove the twelve miles to Belton, with a cake box sitting in the footwell, out of the sun.

I'd managed to find a few spare minutes in my afternoon to make a trip to Myla's bakery. I'd picked a selection of treats after I'd looked at what Linc and River had bought the day before. My stomach growled as I recalled the assortment of cookies and doughnuts inside the box.

My habit of missing a meal had become a frequent thing lately and had caused me to drop a little weight. Not thinking it was a bad thing for my waistline, my Mom had started to worry when I popped by the house. The lasagne I'd fed River and Linc the previous night was proof of her concern.

I pushed up my sunglasses before indicating to switch lanes.

Was Linc's lack of parents who cared about him and Lizzie the reason why he was overprotective of River?

Without children of my own, I had no gauge against which to measure the protective urges Linc had for River, well, except for how my family treated me, so I'd gone searching for answers to see if I could persuade him to listen to reason. What I'd found left my emotions in turmoil as I read through all the information Linda, my secretary, had found in her search. My eyes ached recalling the pictures she'd found of a raid the police had carried out about thirty years prior. Although the picture was a little faded, I'd spotted Linc and Lizzie standing off to one side. Linc had been tall for his age, but he'd been rail thin. His face had looked haunted as he'd clung to the small toddler at his side, his eyes daring anyone to take her from him.

The information on his parents was sparse. It seemed his father had run off around the same time the picture had been taken. His mother had drunk herself to death not long after that. Why hadn't anyone gone in to get those kids out of there?

There were no reports I could find that anyone had tried to help Linc or his sister. It was as if the law hadn't given a fuck about what happened to them. I was pretty sure that's why Linc was suspicious, and rebelled against law enforcement and authority. It also explained why he'd changed after River had been born.

I sighed in defeat, realizing how much of a wall I had to climb to help him, especially as I didn't want to make him do something that went against everything he'd done to keep River safe.

"Fucking hell," I cursed as I exited the highway. When I pulled up onto the empty drive, it was with a heavy heart.

I sat for a moment and looked up at the house Linc had turned into a home for him and River. The ache in my eyes increased and I took off my sunglasses, throwing them on the seat next to me to rub at my eyes.

"You're trying to help him," I muttered under my breath.

Then why does it feel like the exact opposite of that?

There was a tap at my window, causing me to jerk as I looked into Nutty's curious expression.

"You alright?" she asked, loud enough for me to hear.

I grabbed the box off the floor and got out of the car, grateful for the layer of cloud that was covering the sun, even though it still left the muggy heat behind. "Yeah, I'm fine. It's just been a long day is all."

I eyed her bright pink fitted dress and dainty shoes before looking back at her fully made up face. "You got a hot date?"

"I have. So, I gotta be off if I don't wanna be late. See you." She offered me a bright smile as she tottered off toward the garage and disappeared through a side door.

I'd taken no more than ten steps up the path when the front door opened, and River raced out. "I was watchin' for ya." She bounced on the top step, her sunbeam yellow shorts and matching top making her appear brighter than the sun.

"Why thank you, kind lady. It's my real pleasure to escort you to dinner," I said in a deep southern drawl befitting a real southern gentleman.

She giggled and played along, holding out her elbow for me to hook my arm through. I stooped as I reached the top of the porch, linking my arm through hers. My back twinged at the awkward angle, but I led her into the house and up to the apartment as I would a lady at a high-class function.

She then went and spoiled it when we reached the top steps and she hollered, "Poppy, Mason's 'ere."

I chuckled and ran my hand over her plaited hair after she dropped her arm. She eyed the box I held in the other hand. "Did ya bring a treat with ya?"

"I did, but it's for after dinner."

Her face fell for a second, then she got a look I could only imagine that would have the boys, or girls, tripping over themselves for her in a few years.

"Mason, we's never got to eat our treats last night, so maybe we's should eat them first before dinner as not to miss out." She batted long eyelashes at me and gave me a beautiful killer smile.

"Quit it, Spirit. Supper first then treats," came Linc's voice through the open door to the apartment.

I bit the inside of my cheek as she rolled her eyes at me and whispered, "I's be quieter next time I's ask."

I tapped her on the end of her nose, the stress of the day forgotten as I winked at her and whispered back, "You'll get me in trouble with your Poppy."

"That's right, she will," Linc said from the doorway, his voice back to sounding like he'd had a pack of smokes. It was rough and sexy enough to make my whole body react.

A wave of heat rode up my neck that I blamed solely on the heat outside as his gaze swept over me from head to toe and back. "You feeling a little hot there...Mason?"

Sexual energy thrummed through me faster than Stevie Ray Vaughn could strum his guitar strings, making it hard to stand still under his appraisal.

River took my hand and tugged. "Da sun is hot outside, you's better come in to cool off," she encouraged while Linc, the fucker, gave me one of those lazy smiles that left me desperate to kiss him.

Christ almighty, that smile should be fucking outlawed.

"Thanks, River," I muttered, letting her drag me inside as Linc moved to stand back.

As I passed, his eyes held a challenge that left me edgy and needy in ways that weren't fitting in a child's presence. I broke eye contact first and thrust the cake box at him without a word. As he took it, I started to immediately think about crime scene photos that I had in a file on my desk. Only when that did the job of quelling the desire, did I focus back on River.

When Linc went into the kitchen, I let out a sigh of relief, needing a moment or two to gather up my defenses. I listened to River chatter as she mentioned what she'd done that day. Feeling far more relaxed than I could have imagined, I lounged on the couch with her sitting next to me.

The large copper and wood overhead fan stirred the warm air and brought with it the scent of melting cheese. My stomach made an embarrassingly noisy growl.

"Ya belly sounds like Missy Layton's cats fightin'," River stated worriedly, while she eyed my stomach like it might attack her.

"It's a good thing the food is ready then."

I glanced over the back of the couch at Linc and wondered how long he'd been watching us. Saying nothing when River jumped off the couch, I followed suit and got up. When Linc didn't move, but continued to stare at me, I got the urge to make sure I didn't have something stuck to my face.

"What?"

He glanced over his shoulder, then glanced back at me. "If you hurt her, there'll be no place on earth you'll be safe from me, you hear me." The threat was said with deadly intent and I knew he meant every word.

My heart thundered loudly in my ears as a strange tension built between us. It was a hollow victory that he was going to let me use River to help sort out the mess he was in after everything I'd learned about him.

To make him understand that I was as conflicted as he was, I removed the distance between us. My heart led my actions and I laid my hand over his sister's tattoo. His eyes blazed and he froze in place, his chest unmoving under my palm.

I looked him right in the eye, holding his gaze with mine. "If I hurt her, you won't need to come for me, 'cause I'll be at your door deserving everything you dish out." I sucked in a shaky breath. "She's more than just a job…" I left it there, unable to carry on when there was still too much at stake for all of us.

His hand came up and took hold of the mine in a firm grip. "Nobody touches me here but Spirit," he growled, right before he removed my hand off his fast beating heart.

The air backed up in my lungs at the simple action that conveyed so much more than any words could have.

A huge ball of emotion lodged itself in the center of my chest and my Adam's apple bobbed several times before I could utter, "You can trust me."

His dark hair shifted around his shoulders as his head moved. "We'll see."

JP Sayle

Chapter 17

Lincoln

Whatever I'd expected, it hadn't been that Mason would have us in Judge Rains's chambers less than a week after he'd mentioned it. I tapped my fingers on my thigh as I eyed the people around the large table. Mr Winter, Nola's lawyer, and the court appointed official for River, a woman Mason explained would document everything that was discussed, paid me and River no attention.

We'd been waiting on the judge to arrive for the last five minutes, and as they ticked by, the silence grew, and I felt my skin start to itch.

The ball of anxiety in my stomach tightened when River placed her tiny hand over mine and gave it a squeeze. I gave her a tight smile, checking that her summer dress of blue and yellow was still clean and she looked presentable. I'd often not notice when she got messy because kids should be able to get dirty and play without restriction. This, it appeared, was not great for coming to meet a judge. Nutty had explained River needed to look her best today to prove I could care for her.

What did clothes and clean shoes have to do with caring for a child? *Fuck knows!* But I'd done as she'd said, not wanting to give anyone an excuse.

"Poppy, stop scowlin'," River whispered.

"Sorry, Spirit," I muttered back, working on smoothing out my features into a mask of indifference that was the furthest from what I was actually feeling.

Would they believe her? What if they think I set this up?

The call yesterday, and the fear that gnawed at me, had left me with nothing but questions and a foul mood that even River's sunny nature hadn't been able to shift. I hadn't seen Mason since I'd agreed to this ludicrous suggestion. Now, as I watched him with his head down, reading something on the table in front of him, I wondered if it was because he was worried I'd change my mind. Or maybe it was something else? The sexual tension between us seemed to grow each time we met. Was he struggling as much as me to keep his hands to himself?

A door opened behind me and I stiffened. Mason nudged my arm, encouraging me to stand. I swallowed the sigh of disapproval at having to act out of character, and stood.

River took hold of my hand with trembling fingers as she looked at the man moving to take a seat across the table. This time I squeezed, offering her reassurance that everything would be fine. And if it wasn't, then I'd kill Mason, slowly, using my hands.

As if Mason sensed my misgivings and had read my mind, he offered me a confident smile that, for some reason, helped alleviate the tension riding my ass.

A scrawny looking man in a suit, I'd not noticed come in with the judge, spoke. "Please be seated."

Once everyone sat, the judge's gaze swept about the table before landing on Mason. "Mr. Davenport, as it is at your request to have this closed meeting to bring forth evidence that you suggest can dispute the charges against your client, I'll let you take the lead." His tone and facial expression gave nothing away, but his gaze had moved to River and his brows rose ever so slightly.

"Thank you, Judge Rains. As I explained when I contacted your office, a witness has been identified that disputes the allegations Miss Fink has made against my client."

Mr. Winter made a weird grunting sound, but when the judge glanced in his direction, he became silent and Mason continued.

"Due to the sensitive nature of the case and the age of the witness, I felt it was appropriate to do this behind closed doors." As he continued to lay out his reasoning, the judge's gaze went back to River.

River, for the first time, remained still, her eyes firmly fixed on the judge as if understanding this man was important.

When Mason finished speaking, the judge glanced at Mr. Winter. "Do you have anything you'd like to say before I ask River some questions?"

"I'll wait until you've finished, if that suits?" Mr. Winter stated, his voice full of false gratitude.

The judge's eyes narrowed but he didn't reply, instead he looked at River. "River, do you understand why you're here today?" he asked kindly, his voice softening.

River wriggled closer to the table. "I's do. Nola, a bad woman, said things about my Poppy that aren't true. You's want to know what I saw and heard, isn't that right, Mason?" Her gaze moved from the judge to Mason, a big smile sliding over her face when he nodded.

Again, the judge's eyes narrowed thoughtfully as he glanced between Mason and River. What was he thinking? Did he think Mason had got River to lie?

As the questions circled in my head and I struggled to keep from saying something, Judge Rains asked, "River, do you know what the date is today?"

I tensed at the odd question.

"Yes, it's July seventeenff. Nutty helped me learn the dates in da appointment book so I knows when it's okay to go and see Poppy and not interrupt him when he's busy."

"Do you know the date that Miss Fink was at the clubhouse?"

Convinced you could have heard a pin drop, everyone in the room seemed to take a collective breath as River's tiny brow scrunched and she started to count on her fingers.

"We's not been back to the club since dat night, so it would be da twenty-ninff of May. There was a party and when Nutty has a date, I go to the clubhouse with Poppy."

My stomach dropped when Mr. Winter started to write on some paper he had in front of him. Mason, on the other hand, continued to smile at River as if she were doing everything right.

When I brought my attention back to Judge Rains, there was something about his face that, for the first time, allowed my fear to ease, if only a little. Could Mason have been right all along?

"You're doing great, River. Can you tell me what happened that night?"

"Do ya want me to tell ya everything I did dat night? 'Cause, I's not sure I can remember everythin'" she stated, her mouth pinching.

The judge's face showed amusement. "No, you don't need to tell me everything. Just tell me what you remember."

"Oh, ok." She hesitated and reached her hand out to me. I took it and offered her a smile. "I's wasn't happy 'cause Nutty was goin' out and Luna, she's my bestest friend, had been naughty, so I's couldn't go and stay with her." She sniffed. "Poppy took me's to the clubhouse at bedtime. When he putted me to beds, he switched on da monitor thingy that lets him 'ear me if I want him. He's only on the other side of da house, but he likes to know I's can call him."

As she continued to talk about what happened that night, the weasel lawyer lost a little of his color and Mason seemed to find it hard to keep his happiness masked.

My eyes widened as I learned that River was a sponge that soaked up everything she saw and heard.

"Ya see, Nola eyes my Poppy like I look at the sweetie drawer. He's never gonna be interested 'cause Poppy is gay." She glanced away from the judge to me. "Da's the right word, Poppy, isn't it?"

A wave of heat spread up my neck as I worked to keep my embarrassment under control as all eyes, bar Mason's, fixed on me. Mr. Winter's mouth hung open and his eyes were huge as he stared at me.

"That's correct, Spirit," I ground out through my bunched jaw while I made sure to meet everyone's gaze head on. I wasn't ashamed of being gay, I just hated people knowing my personal shit, especially when it could be used as a weapon against me. I'd learned to keep my sexual preferences to myself and, judging by the reaction of all but River and Mason, I'd done a good job.

Judge Rains shifted in his seat, his eyes hardening as he stared directly at me. "Can I ask why this is the first time this information is being shared?"

I shrugged. "What difference does it make? In my experience, you condemn a man just 'cause he's affiliated with Dark Angels."

Feeling the weight of Mason's eyes on me, I ignored him and continued to hold the judge's gaze.

"The reputation and evidence of past crimes speak for themselves, Mr. Stone, but I'd like to believe that *I* let the evidence in a case be the judge." His tone was arctic, and River started to fidget.

Putting River's needs above having it out with the judge, my lips tightened into a thin line and I slouched into the chair, giving off an air of 'whatever.'

Chapter 18

Mason

Cursing Linc for challenging the judge, my grip tightened on the pen I held as I waited to see if this would derail all the hard work I'd done to get this meeting. I'd slept for shit for days, working on the backlog of cases I had during the day, and then going home every evening to work through Linc's case to make sure I'd covered every angle.

What I'd not considered was telling Linc to keep his mouth shut. Had this fucked things up? When Linc slouched into the chair, his 'fuck you' look firmly in place, I had the urge to kick him under the table.

I refrained, but it was a close call when I could see my hard work and effort being for nothing. Instead, I turned my attention to Judge

Rains. "My client's sexual orientation is not the issue here, it's the allegations made against him," I placated.

Hard eyes turned to me and the judge's brows rose. "I'm surprised at you, Mr. Davenport. This is a vital piece of information, is it not? If your client is gay, surely it casts doubt onto what Miss Fink alleges occurred between her and Mr. Stone?"

The muscles in my shoulders tensed to the point they started to ache in protest. "I'll concede that it would seem important in a rape case, but my client likes to keep personal matters private, and had initially hoped that his innocence, rather than his sexual orientation, could resolve the issue." I realized my mistake the moment the words were out of my mouth.

I turned in my seat to look at River, her face was ashen and her eyes were brimming with unshed tears. *Fucking hell! Stupid bastard!*

Before I could utter an apology, Linc was moving to pick River up out of her seat, his face rigid while his eyes blazed at me. My heart stuttered in my chest at the look of disgust he threw at me. *Oh my god, what had I done?*

"Enough," Linc growled.

The judge held his hand up and his face showed sympathy before he spoke. "I understand this is upsetting for River, do you wish to take a break before continuing?"

I could see by Linc's face what his reply would be before he uttered a word. "Mr. Stone would like to request a ten-minute break," I stated, before he could say a word.

The threatening sneer aimed at me caused my heart to sink to the floor, but I didn't back down. With agreement, and a silently seething Linc, we left the room. The busy hall offered no privacy and I sighed as Linc held on to River like a precious gift. Her crestfallen face and sad eyes stabbed at me.

I indicated down the hall to a door that led to a private room lawyers could use to talk to clients during meetings such as the one I'd organized today. "There's a room right down the hall we can use." I hoped it was free as I walked off, hoping Linc would follow.

I breathed a little easier when the sound of his booted feet sounded behind me. The moment the door shut behind us, I faced him. The heat of his gaze stole my breath and I struggled to form an apology that would remove the fury I could see and feel in the small room.

"I'm sorry."

River lifted her arms out toward me before Linc could say a word. "Mason," her chin wobbled, and I stepped toward her.

My hands shook as I opened my arms, waiting to see if I'd broken the fragile trust Linc had given me not even a week earlier. The seconds that ticked by were never ending, before he finally relinquished his hold and River leaned forward for me to take her.

A wave of dizziness swept over me and I had to lock out my knees to keep standing. I buried my nose in her sweet-smelling hair and I held her to my chest. "I'm so sorry, River. I should never have said those things in front of you."

Her small hands came up to rub at my cheeks, watching me with eyes far older than her years. "You's tryin' to protect my Poppy from the bad people. Sometimes we say and hear things dat hurt."

Eyes so much like Linc's turned molten and as she looked over to him. "Don't be mad at Mason, he's gonna save ya Poppy by tellin' da truth. Ya kept secrets from me, and isn't dis what ya say always happens? Da truth always comes out." The stern voice coming from a five-year-old made it hard to remember this wasn't a funny situation.

Raw emotions flitted across Linc's face as he met my gaze over River's head. "I don't need savin', Spirit, but you're right, I should have explained everythin'," he rasped, his voice thick with some unknown emotion I couldn't fathom.

Not sure I'd been forgiven when he refused to meet my gaze, I checked the time. "We need to go back in."

"No more speeches," Linc growled as he took River from me and stalked out of the room.

I caught River's eye roll before the door shut, and I leaned against the wall, working on steadying myself. Had I fucked any chance up with Linc? *You have to close the case first. Then you can beg for forgiveness.*

Exiting the room, I walked slap bang into Mr. Winter, Freddy, to his friends. Not that he and I could ever be classed as that. He was a sleaze, and I'd never go out of my way to befriend the prick. His only goal was to make money and it didn't matter if his clients told the truth or not. His reputation preceded him.

We'd had a few run-ins that left me feeling tainted. To that end, I'd made it my mission to avoid him. The only thing was, he was also gay and had made no bones about how he'd like to bounce on my bone.

His face held an ugly sneer that he probably thought was a come on. "I can now see why you'd be interested in defending Mr. Stone. He'd be a prize in anyone's trophy cabinet."

The people roaming the hall around us faded into the background as anger pulsed through my veins. My fists balled at my sides as

I took a step closer to him and glowered. "I'd mind your fucking mouth. That man deserves respect, something you know very little about."

His face showed fear for a second before the sneer was back. "Oh, you've got it bad. He must be a good fuck—"

My hand reached out to grab hold of his shirt front and tug him close enough I could smell his stale breath as I shut him down. "If you utter one more word about Mr. Stone, that ten-thousand-dollar smile will be situated somewhere at the back of your head," I ground out through clenched teeth.

I shook him once, before releasing him to spin around only to be met by Linc and River, who stood not ten feet from me. Both expressions showed they'd not missed the exchange. I sighed when heat spread over my face.

River recovered first. "Dat told him! He's a nasty man with eyes likes a weasel."

I choked back my laughter as Mr. Winter stomped off. I paid him no mind when I caught an odd look in Linc's eyes, and my laughter died. Had I just made things worse between us?

Not wanting to dwell on how I'd been fucking things up, I checked my watch again. "We'd better get back in before they send a search party for us."

Linc's brooding gaze lingered for a moment before he nodded, and we all walked back to the door we'd exited ten minutes earlier.

Back in our seats, Judge Rains continued where he'd left off with his questioning. Sweat soaked the back of my shirt by the time we'd finished. The sense that River had swayed the tide grew with every question she answered. Her voice rang with truth. She didn't falter and kept her story consistent, even when Mr. Winter had tried to trip her up.

At the end of his questions, his face was a mask of frustration, whereas the judge looked more than a little pleased. He'd offered River a warm smile and thanked her for her testimony.

"Dat's alright, Judge. Poppy says you's have to tell da truth otherwise nothin' good happens." Her brow pinched as she looked between the judge and Mr. Winter. "Will ya make Nola and that nasty man pay for not's tellin' the truth?"

The judge choked back a laugh as his face went a little red. His eyes gleamed with amusement before he could pull himself together. "I'll need to go through all the evidence from today and weigh what action I need to take." His answer was noncommittal, but River seemed pleased with it, nonetheless.

"Thank you, Judge," she offered her tiny hand to him and he got up and reached across the table to take it.

"You're welcome, and it was a pleasure to meet you, River."

Linc's brows arched up, and I kept my lips in a straight line, gathering my things after the judge advised we were to return the following day for his verdict.

Outside, dark clouds hung heavy in the sky, threatening a storm after the heat and humidity of the last couple of weeks.

River stood next to Linc, bouncing on the pavement. "Are we's goin' for ice cream now, Poppy? Ya promised me."

Linc gave her the first genuine smile I'd seen all afternoon before he glanced at me. I stilled as he stared at me with the same look he'd given me after I'd chewed out Mr. Winter.

"You wanna come for ice cream?" His voice was gruff and uncertain.

The gaze that held mine for a second revealed vulnerability that left my heart thudding madly against my ribs. I winked at them both. "It just so happens I love ice cream."

When his shoulders visibly relaxed, the final knots that had formed after my outburst about the allegations, released and, for a moment, I let myself believe that he'd forgiven my fuck up.

Chapter 19

Lincoln

As I walked out of the court building the following day, without the tracker attached to my ankle, I couldn't help but look at the man who'd worked to make it happen. His hair moved in the fresh breeze the storm had left in its wake as his thoughtful eyes met mine and the air became trapped in my lungs.

I'd not wanted to admit that a part of me had doubted he'd pull this off, yet here I stood on the sidewalk, a free man. The judge had waffled a load of stuff I'd not really listened to until he'd pinned Mr. Winter with a hard stare, advising him that his client could find herself on the wrong side of the law if I chose to press charges against her for false accusations, defamation of character, and a bunch of other crap I wasn't interested in.

No, she'd be dealt with just like the other treacherous bastards, by the rules of the club. If she wanted to be a prospect, then she'd find out what that could mean to someone like her. As for the other members who'd tried to gain control of the club, it was time to pay them a little visit.

Mason had warned me that Mr. Winter had probably already alerted Nola to what had happened yesterday. I wasn't worried. There was nothing she could say to Ned that might alert him to what I'd found out.

"Listen, I've got to head back to the office…I was…erm wondering…maybe you and River…would like to come over to my parents for another barbecue on Sunday. No pressure," he finished lamely, his face full of hope he didn't hide.

The invitation answered a question I'd asked myself last night. Once Mason had done his job, would he wash his hands of me, or still be interested?

I'd heard what he'd said to Winter after I'd come out of the restroom with River, and even with my anger still boiling inside me at his outburst in front of River, I had to recognize that he'd cut the fucker down to size for me.

Had a man ever treated me with real respect that didn't come with the knowledge of the club and who I was? I couldn't think of one time, and that right there scared the fuck out of me. This man, I'd somehow known, was different than anyone I'd encountered before. He had a code of ethics that was hard to match.

Could I trust him, not only with me, but River, too? We were a package deal that came with more baggage than most and I wasn't stupid to assume that just because Mason was attracted to me now, that he'd want more.

He must have taken my silence for refusal when he muttered, "Okay then, well you have my number if there's—"

"Yes."

His brows rose. "Yes? Yes to you have my number, or yes to Sunday?" The hope was back on his face and I cursed under my breath, finding myself defenseless against his openness.

"Yes to all of it," I muttered as a wave of heat coursed through me at the sexy smile that formed on his far too tempting lips.

"You have the address. It kicks off about one. Do you want me to come and pick you and River up? Then you can have a few beers. I can have someone drop you both home when you're ready to leave." His sea-green eyes gleamed in the sunlight and I found myself nodding.

I felt more than a little awkward as I stood there, fighting the urge to kiss the smug smile off his lips. "Later," I muttered, walking away before I gave in to temptation.

Back in the parking lot, I sat astride my Harley, strapping my open face helmet on. I slipped my Oakley's out of the front of my leather jacket and put them on. Taking several deep breaths, I savored the sense of freedom and the lack of metal around my ankle. The engine throbbed to life as I turned the ignition.

A grin spread over my lips. *Time to clean the house.*

☠ ☠ ☠

My first stop was the auto shop. The sound of my bike must have alerted Sid because he appeared from inside the large garage as I came to halt on the front drive.

His face was smeared with grease, as was his bald head. His blue overalls weren't in a much better condition as he strolled toward me, rubbing his hand on a greasy rag. I acknowledged his presence before glancing at the sparkling clean window with a display of bikes. The artwork on the frames and tanks made me itch to get a closer look.

With most of my time taken up with the tattoo shop and club business, I didn't come to the auto shop often. This was Sid's baby, and he'd run it for the last ten years. He was always coming up with new ideas to keep the business fresh, and what I was looking at was the latest addition.

Where there had once been corrugated iron, in its place was a large wall of glass. The small part of the shop he'd turned into a showroom had white walls that made the bikes and the artwork stand out. "You clever fuck, that artwork sings against the white."

I got off my bike and strolled to him, slapping him on the back as he gave me a grin.

"What can I say, I'm a genius." He glanced over at the window. "I've even asked Toad to work on a design for my bike."

"No fucking way! You're gonna let someone loose on your hog?" I could hear the disbelief in my voice as my gaze moved from the window back to Sid. "In all the time we've been friends, not once have you let anyone touch your bike."

He shrugged as if it wasn't a big issue, though I knew it was a huge deal. He'd been known to threaten to kill anyone that breathed anywhere near his bike. "He's a fucking master, man, what can I say?"

His voice held an awe I wasn't used to hearing come from him, and my gaze narrowed on him.

"You got a thing for him?" Sid was gay, but it was a touchy subject and one I didn't often mention for want of not getting a punch in the face.

He stilled before he forcibly appeared to relax his stance. "It's not up for discussion," he said, shutting me down, so I let it go.

Instead, I lifted up my jean leg to reveal my ankle. His eyes darkened and a malicious smile formed. The knuckles of the hand holding the rag turned white as he lifted his fist. "It's time to show them why you're president."

My gaze narrowed on the open workshop door behind Sid, and the shadow of a man who wasn't quick enough to move back before I'd seen him. "Did ya talk to Ram?"

"I did. He'll keep his mouth shut if he knows what's good for him. Beau, he's too full of his own importance to notice anything." As Sid spoke, he glanced back at the workshop.

"That'll work in our favor." He twisted his head to look back at me. "When you wantin' to set the wheels in motion." His knuckles cracked.

"Let's stick to the plan. Now that Mason has managed to work his magic, I don't wanna end up back inside. Revenge is best served cold," I ground out, my jaw aching as my teeth clenched. The plan was to wait for the next ride out, which was planned in a month's time. I'd had Sid reach out on my behalf, so as not to breach the terms of my bail, to an old club member, Rattlesnake.

Quinn, aka Rattlesnake, had originally come from Austin. He'd followed an old flame to Belton, but when they'd split up and he'd lost his job, he'd decided to head back to Austin. I had affiliations with The Chosen Few, a club that was based on the far side of Austin in Round Rock, so I'd spoken to Dog, the president. He'd accepted Rattlesnake as a prospect at the time.

That had been two years ago. Now Rattlesnake was part of Dog's trusted inner circle. When that had happened earlier this year, Dog had offered me a favor for sending Rattlesnake his way. I'd gotten Sid to call in that favor and it seemed once Sid had laid out what had happened, Dog was only too happy to help.

I rubbed at my bristly jaw. "If everything goes to plan, then the fall out shouldn't touch the club, or us."

"I don't fucking care if it touches me, right now all I want is to make sure that none of those traitors walk, or ride a fucking bike again," he growled, low and mean.

"Amen to that, but we can't show our hand right now, got it?"

"Yeah, yeah, that don't mean I gotta like it." Red splotches of color appeared over his cheekbones.

I slapped at his arm in a comradely gesture. "Me either, but it will be worth the wait to see that fuckin' light dawn in their eyes when they receive club justice. Hang on to that. Now let's get out of this roasting sun and stop wasting good air on those fuckers. Show me those bikes, I'm thinkin' I might need a new paint job myself."

He chuckled and I knew he'd let it go for now.

Now I just needed to make sure I kept a lid on my own anger for the next four weeks. I heaved a sigh as I followed him into the workshop, wondering for the first time if club business could fuck up something I'd yet to fully accept—my growing feelings for Mason.

Chapter 20

Mason

The sun was already doing its best to melt the asphalt as the heat shimmered and warm air blasted my face through the open window. Stevie Ray Vaughn belted out of the speakers as I drove from Killeen to Belton to collect Linc and River, nerves making my stomach trip over itself.

I took my eyes off the road for a second to glance down. I swallowed a groan, recalling how many outfits I'd tried on before opting for board shorts and a T-shirt. The hope was that I could talk Linc into my parents' pool at some point throughout the afternoon. The heat today would warrant cooling off and gave me a perfect excuse to get close to a wet and semi-naked Linc.

Warmth that had nothing to do with the sun spread down my body and I squeezed my butt and shifted. *Come on, you're picking up a child!*

That thought did little to help my problem. It had been getting progressively harder to think about anything other than Linc since I'd left him on the court steps. With the last time he'd been in my parents' home on replay, I stood little chance of keeping hold of the desire.

Did I want to be his bitch? I fully understood what that meant to Linc, but I tended to top in my relationships, not that I'd had one in a while. That being said, I was not averse to letting Linc fuck me. My ass clenched and my dick jerked against the front of my shorts, seemingly happy with the idea. Yet, I knew myself, I'd never be content with that being the only option.

Getting a little ahead of yourself, aren't you?

You've kissed once. Maybe Linc isn't up for more.

Choosing not to let that depressing thought linger, I hit the gas pedal, focusing on the fact he'd agreed to come to the barbecue. That had to mean something, right?

Oh fuck, stop! You're acting like a teenager going out on his first date.

The fact I'd thought about little else over the last three days, waiting not so patiently for Sunday to arrive, was a little more needy than

I'd like. This was our first real date. Did he see this as a date?

I chewed my lower lip between my teeth. Had I made it clear I saw this as a date? *Shit!* Did he think this was just a 'celebration of winning the case' kind of thing? I cursed long and loud as I hit Belton city limits and followed the signs. Why hadn't I made it clear?

With no real answers to my internal debate, I pulled into Linc's drive. A smile spread over my face at the sight of River sitting on the porch with a large colorful bag next to her.

She waved when she realized it was me and was shouting loud enough for me to hear. "Poppy, Mason's 'ere."

I chuckled as I stepped out of the car. Leaving the door open, I headed up the drive to meet River, who was trying to lift the large bag with difficulty. "Wanna hand, sweetie?" As I took hold of the bag that weighed a ton, I glanced up at the sound of feet walking over the wooden floor.

A loud buzzing started in my ears, and my tongue suddenly found itself glued to the roof of my mouth. Holy fuck!

Up till now, Linc had only ever worn jeans, and although he looked mighty fine in them, Linc dressed in low slung cut-offs that revealed tanned, muscled legs covered in fine dark hair was a wet dream. Combine that with a T-shirt of deep plum that clung lovingly to his chest, and hair that had been pulled back and put into a makeshift bun. On many, it would look wrong, but on him it made him look even sexier.

Inappropriate images of holding on to the bun while he fucked me against some hard surface ran through my head. My body instantly reacted, and a flush of embarrassment rode up my neck. *Child, there's a child right there!*

As if he knew where my thoughts had gone, he looked at River and raised a brow. His now golden eyes gleamed with humor and, if I wasn't mistaken, desire while his lips quirked up. "You're lookin' a little hot and bothered there, Mase, you feelin' alright?"

I was thrown for a second by him shortening my name. My mouth opened then closed. Was that a term of endearment? *Jeez, you're acting like a stupid fool, pull it together.*

It took effort to stop myself slapping at my forehead as I met Linc's amused gaze. "It's hotter than hell out here."

"Then whats we waitin' for?" River asked impatiently as she tugged at the hand not holding the bag I'd forgotten I was still gripping.

"What the heck have you got in here? It feels like you have everything but the kitchen sink," I said to hide my nerves.

"Lots of things I might need. I's didn't 'ave my swimmers last time, so I's put them in the bag. And I's a towel, sunscreen, a hat, a present for your Mom and Dad. Oh, and some food Poppy made. We's got to be social, isn't dat right Poppy?" She looked expectantly up at Linc, and this time, it was his turn for color to flood his face.

"Yeah...I thought we were in a rush to get movin'."

He sounded uncomfortable as I eyed him. "Everything okay?" The question in my eyes asked if he were having second thoughts about today.

My heart thrummed against my ribs when he came toward me, his hand coming up to grip the back of my neck. His gaze held mine for what felt the longest time before he lowered his lips to mine. This kiss was so different from the first. It was light and gentle, but the impact was no less forceful. I felt it through my whole being. The lazy way his lips explored mine left me breathless and needy by the time his mouth left mine. There was a promise in the depths of his eyes that made it a little easier to step back and not demand he kiss me again.

"Oh, dat was lovely, Poppy. Ya made Mason's eyes go all dreamy."

If I'd thought I was hot before, I now felt like I'd had my head in a furnace as River pointed out how dopey I looked. I coughed and muttered, "Right…let's get going then."

Rich, full laughter followed me as I walked back to the car with as much dignity as I could muster. By the time Linc had transferred River's booster seat into the back of my car and was happy she was safe, my embarrassment had faded.

The drive back to Killeen flew by as River chatted excitedly about seeing Declan again. Linc remained silent, but he appeared relaxed in a way I'd not seen before. His usual dominant aura was there, but it appeared to be dialed back a few notches. I was more than pleased to note his face had lost its pinched, strained look.

His head twisted toward me, though the dark Oakley glasses prevented me from seeing his eyes. "Shouldn't you be watchin' the road?"

The low, sexy timbre of his voice caused a shiver to race down my spine, regardless of the heat. I turned my attention back to the windshield, focusing on the road and saying nothing.

When I was tempted to look back at him, I gripped the steering wheel and chanted internally *'watch the road, watch the road.'*

It was harder than I wanted to admit, with him sitting so temptingly close and smelling like heaven. His scent was dark and a little dangerous, like him, and far too tempting in the small confines of the car, even with the windows open.

By the time we arrived at my parents and walked into their air-conditioned home, I was more than ready to beg for mercy. To beg for two minutes alone with Linc to...well, do whatever as long as he was touching me.

Without the legal obligations coming between us, my head had finally caught up with what my body wanted. It was in joint agreement. It wanted a naked Linc any way I could get him.

"What you thinkin' 'bout?" Linc whispered into my ear, his hot breath touching my cheek while warmth radiated off his body behind me.

I tensed and struggled to act naturally while my gut churned with need. I twisted my head and River caught my attention as she hopped from one foot to another. When I met Linc's heavy-lidded gaze, I had to swallow twice before answering.

"I'll show you later." His nostrils flared and his lips moved into that lazy smile that turned my insides to jelly.

"I'll look forward to it."

I wasn't sure if I was happy or not when my brother, Hudson, saved me from saying anything more.

"It's about time you turned up, if Dec had asked me once more what time River was coming, I might have strangled him." His voice was full of humor as he pulled me in for a one-armed hug and then nodded to Linc, his face still in a friendly smile. "It's good to see you again, Lincoln. If you have time later, I'd like to talk about getting another tattoo." His voice dropped and he glanced about the empty hallway before carrying on, "But don't mention it in front of the wife."

Linc lips quirked up and he shook his head, "You're pussy-whipped."

Hudson burst out laughing and River shook her head. "Poppy, ya say I's not allowed to say bad words. I's sure that's one."

There was the sound of feet clattering over the wood before Declan appeared through the open lounge door. "River, River ya's 'ere. C'mon on, I gots a new water float for da pool to play with." In a flurry, River disappeared through the house with Declan.

Chapter 21

Lincoln

I stood listening to Hudson rag on Mason. Looking at Mason's cheeky grin, I shoved my hands into my short pockets to hide my reaction. The moment I'd stepped out of my house, the sexual energy had burst to life under my skin. When I'd been standing on the porch, Mason hadn't concealed his attraction and it had steamrollered right over my good intentions to behave today.

There was no excuse for kissing his sweet mouth. Fuck, I'd been more desperate to kiss him than I'd been to have the metal tag off my leg. It scared the shit out of me and made the three days of trying to talk myself out of doing anything hasty utterly useless. I'd no restraint against Mason's sea-green gaze that begged for things that I had no business wanting.

The moment our mouths touched, I'd been lost in him. Lost in the need to touch, to taste, to feel, to surround myself with him. Any and all thoughts of waiting to start something after the plans I'd set in motion for retribution were resolved, had been blown apart by the sweetness of the moment.

I don't do sweet.

Says who? You loved it, so stop fucking lying to yourself.

In all my years, I couldn't remember ever being driven by desire this strong before. *Fuck*, if it didn't change everything. I wasn't sure I was ready for what it meant, but I'd be damned if I could stop myself from taking what Mason was offering.

When Hudson knocked my shoulder with his in a friendly gesture, I realized I'd zoned out and wasn't quite sure what I'd missed after River had darted off with Declan.

"You up for it?" asked Hudson, his brows arched as he waited for me to answer.

"Sorry, up for what?" I didn't look at Mason when he snorted and choked back his laughter.

"Up for a game of water volleyball? We're one man down and I think you'll be a good match against the slippery eel over there," Hudson nodded at Mason, who gave him a toothy grin.

"You'll never beat me, bro, you need to give up trying."

"We'll see about that. I think Lincoln might be up to the job?" Hudson eyed me and gave a subtle wink.

At a complete loss on how to respond, I gave a curt nod.

All of my life, I'd only ever been included in things by those connected to the club. The only real relationship I'd had as a child had been with Lizzie. I'd never formed friendships or been included in anything at school. No one ever bothered because of who I was associated with. Most of my childhood had been spent as the outcast, the one that people picked on. That was, until I'd started to shoot up in size, grow some muscle, and fight back. This being asked to join in a fun activity left me feeling way out of my depth.

Mason laid a hand on my arm and gently squeezed it before he gave me a devilish smirk. "Be prepared to be humiliated if you pick Hudsons team," he cackled wickedly, making Hudson roll his eyes and punch at his arm.

"Fuck off. You'll see, I can tell Lincoln's got skills. Anyway, you always pair up with Luis, that leaves me odd man out." He eyed me again, only this time he looked a little more apprehensive.

"There's only one way to find out." I arched my brow and indicated with my head for Mason to lead on.

An hour later, dripping wet and out of breath, I clung to the side of the pool, laughing as Hudson dunked Mason. We'd won by one shot and it had been a harder fight than I'd ever have imagined. Stupidly thinking it would just be a fun game of water volleyball, I'd soon realized how competitive the brothers were.

I'd found myself ducking more than once when the ball came sailing at my head. They were ruthless and not opposed to underhanded tactics to stop their opponents. Mason had somehow gotten close enough to touch me any opportunity he could and made it real difficult to keep thoughts of bending him over the side of the pool and teaching him a lesson in just my head.

"You'll definitely need to be on my team the next time you come over with Mason," Hudson stated breathlessly as he rested his forearms on the edge of the pool next to me.

The easy acceptance of our somewhat budding relationship was just plain weird. More used to fuck buddies or hook-ups that didn't involve more than me sticking my dick in them, this thing with Mason's family left me uncertain of my footing. I was fucking forty-years-old, and families as nice as the Davenport's would normally run a mile from the likes of me. This whole family acceptance thing was something that would take a bit of getting used to.

What's to say you'll be with him long enough to get used to it? With no wish to answer that, I put a smile on my face. About to respond to Hudson, Mason burst out of the water next to Hudson and sprayed us both.

Hudson choked out a laugh as he wiped at his dripping face, but I gave chase as Mason dived back under the water to swim off. I'd learned to swim in the creek out by the clubhouse, and though I wasn't as fast as Mason, my arms were longer, and I managed to grab his ankle. He didn't put up much resistance as I pulled him toward me under the water. His eyes were alight with humor and desire and I realized what he'd been up to.

When my lungs refused to let me stay under the water another second, I clasped Mason to my chest and kicked up to the surface. Water streamed down his hair and over his face. Droplets caught on his eyelashes as the sun gleamed down and made them sparkle like little diamonds.

I sucked in a shaky breath and struggled not to give in to the desire to kiss him.

"Inside, now," he murmured, low enough that only I could hear.

Not needing to be asked twice, I let him go and concentrated on reigning in my desire, aware there were too many people watching us. Getting out of the pool with a raging hard-on in front of the kids and Mason's family just wasn't something anyone needed to see.

"I'm just gonna show Linc where he can get changed out of his wet suit," Mason shouted at no one in particular as he got out of the pool.

Swallowing the groan when his ass flexed right in my face, I heaved myself out of the pool, keeping my body at an angle out of folk's eyeline.

"Yeah, yeah, whatever you say, son. Remember the food will be ready in ten," his Dad shouted from the grill, his face only showing humor as he continued turning the meat.

My gaze swept the poolside and found River sat in the shade of a large yellow umbrella with Declan and Mason's mom. The table in front of them was covered with books and pens. River paid me no attention as she carried on talking to Declan, her face beaming with happiness. There was a sweet ache in my chest as I glanced back at Mason, who remained in front of me, watching.

"I thought we were going to dry off?" The gruffness couldn't be helped, and Mason took hold of my hand, intertwining our fingers before he squeezed.

The moment lengthened, neither of us saying anything as the anticipation grew between us. A loud shout coming from behind broke the tension. Mason sighed and tugged me over to a sun lounger, grabbing a couple of the towels his Mom had left there for us to use.

Remaining silent, we entered the house and he shut the door behind us. The music and sound of voices lessened. His eyes met mine, the invitation clear.

Emotions I didn't want to think about right then surged through me. I kept hold of his hand and slowly lowered my lips. His mouth tasted of chlorine as my tongue swept over the seam of his lips, encouraging him to open for me. The second he did, the world became an array of color. Bright and bold like the mouth I was kissing, it left me sinking into a pool of desire so deep, I wasn't sure I'd ever have the strength to pull my head back above the water.

A shudder ran down my spine as he moved and his wet, slippery skin touched my chest. The hand holding mine tightened as he groaned low and deep.

"Upstairs...we need...to go upstairs...someone might come in," he panted against my mouth.

"Then move it," I ground out through clenched teeth as I struggled to think straight with his wet body flush against mine.

He was off and running the second the words left my mouth, his hand refusing to let go of mine as he tried to drag me up the stairs. In the time it took to get to a room I'd not been in before, he was breathless. The second the door closed, he was on me. We fell hard against the wall next to the door, my back thudding noisily as we hit. The air left my chest, but I didn't complain as Mason wrapped his firm, slick body around mine. Our mouths met in a hungry kiss and his hands came up, his fingers digging into the bun at the back of my head, holding on.

"When you came out of your house earlier, I imagined you fucking me while I held on to this bun," he rasped before his lips trailed over my jaw to my ear.

The visual filled my head and hardened my cock till it throbbed painfully. Fucking hell, what was he trying to do to me?

Hot breath touched my damp skin and shivers rippled through my body. My cock pressed firmly against Mason's hip as his magic mouth worked to destroy my control. My hands roamed over his damp skin toward his ass. His murmurs of encouragement continued as his lips teased and tormented me, while the heat of his body dried mine, but made my cock leak.

"We don't have enough time, but fuck, I want you." He sounded so disappointed, it helped to take the edge off the needy desperation his actions were causing.

"I'm gonna make you pay for this. You get that, right?" His response was to groan and to grind his own arousal against mine as he shifted so they aligned.

"God, I hope so," he gasped, then his mouth was back on mine. Sizzling heat spread through my whole body till I felt I'd combust. His hips started a sexy roll that mimicked him fucking me, and for the first time in my life, I wanted it. I wanted to feel him inside me, to know what it was like to be owned by another.

As it registered, I lifted my head, my ears buzzing as I stared down at hooded, tempestuous eyes that sucked me into their depths like a stormy sea. If I wasn't careful, I'd be out of my depth before I knew it.

You already are!

Before I could move further away, his hands shifted from my hair and he cupped my cheeks. His eyes implored me...my heart stuttered, and I laid my forehead against his. "You don't wanna be pinning your hopes on more with me. I'm not what you need in your life." The words hurt but they still needed to be said.

His eyes flashed with determination as his fingers tightened. "I get to choose what's good for me. I'm not stupid, I know who and what you're involved in. That makes no difference to me."

I shook my head to dislodge his hands. "You know nothin about my life. About what is required of me."

He took a step back then another as his eyes raked me from top to toe. "I know you've suffered. I know that the club has been the only life you've known. The only family you've ever experienced. I want to show you that you can have more. I can give you more if you'll let me share what I have." His voice cracked, but he kept me pinned with his gleaming eyes. "Give me a chance, please?"

What did I have to offer? Didn't he get I was tainted? That it would never be any different? The question pounded at the sliver of hope that had started to grow when he'd openly offered more.

His eyes continued to beg unashamedly, and the hope inside me seemed to grasp on to my heart, refusing to be ground out. My chest heaved and my temples throbbed. All the desire

I'd felt was gone as I considered if I could for once put myself first.

As if he sensed me weakening, Mason came closer. He didn't touch, but his eyes lowered to my chest before coming to meet my gaze. What I saw stole my breath.

"The only people that have touched your heart are Lizzie and River. I want to be added to that list. I'll go at your pace. I'll do this any way you want"—his eyes darkened—"but I'm not giving up." His mouth slammed against mine in a brutal kiss that was over before it even began, and then he was gone.

Sensations bombarded my body while my brain tried to re-engage. How the fuck was I supposed to fight when he didn't play fair?

JP Sayle

Chapter 22

Mason

"Do you have the file I need for the Carter case? I can't seem to find it." I asked as I came out of my office.

Linda glanced up from her computer, her face blank for a moment. "Sorry, erm, I think I filed it after you said you were finished with it." She shrugged her slim shoulders, but her gaze had already returned to the computer, her hands back to typing.

Used to her behavior, I didn't take offense as I walked past her desk and went to the filing cabinets that were coded in alphabetical order. I opened the drawer I needed and plucked out the file.

"You want to talk about what's on your mind?" Linda asked as I turned to go back to my office.

I glanced at the top of her sunny blonde head. "Why are you asking me that?"

Her gaze moved from the screen to me, and her brows rose. "It might be that normally you never leave your man cave for a file. Instead, you pick up the contraption on your desk called a phone and ask me to bring you what you need." Her voice was laced with humor and her eyes twinkled with mirth.

Was I that easy to read? Linda had been my personal assistant ever since I'd joined the firm. I'd come to rely on her and would often use her as a sounding board when I needed to talk through something. I'd just never used her for my own personal shit. But the option of using my family was out because...well, I just didn't want to talk to them yet about what I felt for Linc, until I'd figured it all out in my own head.

My best friend, Zack, was currently off trying to find himself in some remote part of the world after an epic break-up with who he thought was the love of his life. It turned out said 'love' was banging any dude that moved, in their bed while Zack was working his ass off to pay for the roof over their heads.

My lawyer colleagues/acquaintances were a no go as having a relationship, even with a former client, could still be frowned upon. I eyed Linda as she continued to stare at me expectantly. I sighed and spun around, shouting over my shoulder, "We'll need to talk in my office."

She muttered something I didn't catch, but she got up and came after me. Her heels made no noise on the thick carpet. Heels that she was never without as she said they made her feel like she could take on the world. I wasn't quite sure how, when they mostly looked like they just hurt her feet. Today's pair was ruby red with a spike heel of about four inches. They matched the skirt she wore.

"Okay, spill. What's on your mind?" she demanded the minute she sat in the seat in front of my desk and crossed her slim legs, one foot bouncing continuously. Her attractive face showed a little concern as she searched my face for answers.

"Linc Stone..."

"Yes?"

"I...you see...I—"

"Jeez, you're a lawyer. Speaking is a vital part of your job. What turned you into a stuttering idiot?"

"Hey, I'm your boss, I'm pretty sure you're not supposed to call me a stuttering idiot," I grumbled, though she was right. Her shoulders shrugged and she showed no remorse. "Anyway, I've...feelings for Linc."

Verbalizing the words gave them true meaning and for the first time in my life, I realized I was in a position where someone had the power to crush my heart. I wasn't sure, if I'd been standing, I could have remained upright when my legs felt like jelly. Having a moment of panic, I sucked in a shaky breath. I'm fucked. What if he chooses to leave things as I left them?

Yesterday, he'd come down dressed in his shorts and sat with River, his brooding gaze giving me no clues as to what he was thinking. For a while, I'd thought he'd make an excuse to leave early after I'd laid out how I wanted a relationship with him. But no, he'd stayed but kept his distance from me. I'd given him space while he'd spent some time talking with my dad. When Hudson had offered to drop him and River home, he'd accepted without even looking at me.

That was fifteen hours ago, and I'd heard nothing from him, not that I'd expected to, but that still didn't stop the hope he might have reached out.

Linda's expression was hard to read as she stared at me, the silence lengthening.

"Aren't you going to say something?" I asked, twisting my hands together on the desk in front of me.

"What do you want me to say? That he's got more baggage than a carousel in an airport? That he's all wrong for you? That the club he's mixed up in could compromise you and your position?"

"Thanks for laying that all out for me." I got up and spun around to look at the bright blue sky outside the window. "Don't you think I've thought of all those things?" I ground out through clenched teeth. It was all I could think about last night when I'd gotten home, without lust clouding my mind.

I ran my hands through my hair before turning back to face her. "How do you tell your heart that it's looking at the wrong man?"

"If I had the answer to that I'd be a very rich woman."

My brows rose.

"Sorry, I couldn't resist. But seriously, regardless of what I mentioned, there is something about him that tugs at the heartstrings. The way he cares for that little girl shows that he has the capacity to love and love hard." She got up and came toward me, her face utterly serious. "Love is a tricky bastard that doesn't listen to reason. I've known you a long time and you're a very good judge of character. If you have feelings for Lincoln, then he must be worthy of them." Her hand touched my shirt sleeve. "If you're serious about him, then let your heart lead and don't give up on him. He strikes me as a man that needs someone like you in his life to show him that he can have more than what he's been given in the past."

A ball of emotion lodged in my throat at the picture of Linc, age ten, looking sad and alone, clinging to his sister. Determination I'd displayed to Linc yesterday before I'd left him in my childhood bedroom, came back. I can do this! I can show him I'm worth his time, worth the effort and fear.

Linda's face formed into a smile and she nodded. "There's the Mason I know. Go get 'em tiger."

Laughter rumbled up my chest. "Seriously, go get 'em tiger?"

She chuckled. "It sounded better in my head. Are we done? I have a pile of work my tyrant boss will want this afternoon for court?"

I waved her off, "Go on...and thank you."

"You're welcome," she answered softly before leaving the room.

I sat back behind my desk, my head going over my calendar, trying to figure out when I could pay Linc a surprise visit.

It took two days of working extra hours before I could finish early enough and head over to Linc's tattoo shop. I'd refrained from sending him a message to see if he'd reach out first. He hadn't, but I'd not been deterred. Instead, I'd enlisted the help of River and Nutty. A smile spread over my face. They'd been more than happy to help and informed me that Linc had been worse than a bear with a sore paw over the last couple of days.

I hoped it was because of me, but I couldn't be sure with Miss Fink mouthing off to anyone who would listen about the injustice of the case being thrown out of court. When I'd phoned Nutty the day before to see what Linc had on his schedule for today in the shop, she'd been madder than a swarm of bees getting ready to defend their hive. It would seem, Miss Fink wasn't giving up her quest to put Lincoln away. I'd contacted Mr. Winter on Linc's behalf and had a word about his client, threatening a libel action if she continued to spread her lies.

Whether she listened, only time would tell, but I was going to talk to Linc about it because it had to be affecting his business. Although when I drove past his shop and struggled to find a parking space on his street, it seemed business was as busy as ever.

The wall of heat as I exited the car made me grateful I'd remembered to bring a pair of shorts and a T-shirt to change into. I reached into the back of the car for the picnic basket I'd had Myla's bakery make up for me. I'd added some beers that Nutty told me were Linc's favorite, along with some soft drinks for River and me.

I'd done a little research on Belton, and Stillhouse Lake, situated not far from Linc's home, had four parks with lake access. They offered many amenities that included picnic areas and designated sandy beaches. My hope was to persuade Linc to come for a late afternoon picnic. River was already onboard and Nutty had told me Linc always finished early on Thursdays to spend time with River.

Everything was in place. I just needed to get Linc to agree, simple. Then why did my stomach feel like hundreds of butterflies had taken flight in there?

Chapter 23

Lincoln

River danced at the side of me. "You got ants in your pants or somethin'?"

Her face pinked and she glanced at the open door of my work room. "No, I's…you's supposed to be finished. Ya takin' forever to clean up," she whined, her eyes darting back to the doorway.

Was I missing something? I stopped clearing my stuff away and crouched down in front of her. "You got something on your mind, Spirit?"

The pink of her cheeks went a deep rose and glowed as she evaded looking me in the eye. My heart rate increased. The last couple of days, I'd been aware of the short fuse I'd had on my temper. I blamed Mason for fucking with my head, but that was no excuse for hurting River's feelings. I ran a finger over her warm cheek and encouraged her to look at me. "Have I done something to upset you?"

She threw her arms around my neck and buried her face in my hair. "Oh, Poppy, you's not upset me."

"Then what is it that has you so jumpy?"

She stiffened in my arms and my heart was back to hammering against my ribs.

"Knock knock, am I interrupting?" Mason's voice inquired from behind me and I wobbled as I tried to shift to look over at him.

The air in the room seemed to disappear as he gave me a beautiful smile, which didn't help my already fast beating heart. My gaze swept over him and my body started to react. Before I could move, River released me and spun around to run to Mason, her arms outstretched.

"Ya 'ere…" The sound of her hand slapping against her face was enough for me to register what she'd said.

My eyes narrowed on the pair of them. Was this a setup? Had River known that Mason was coming today? I stood slowly and faced both Mason and River, who had matching sheepish expressions.

"Someone wanna tell me what's goin' on and *why* Mason is here?"

"We's all goin' for a picnic at Stillhouse Lake, aren't we, Mason?" River said excitedly while looking at Mason for confirmation. I didn't miss Mason wince. Clearly River wasn't supposed to spill the beans quite yet.

My brow furrowed. "And whose idea was this?"

"Why Mason's, of course. He's gonna take us on a date, Poppy. My very first date." She sighed, her eyes bright as she rested her head on Mason's shoulder.

There was no way I could deny her, not when she put it like that, and the fucker Mason knew it. I met his unrepentant stare and couldn't find it in me to curse.

I was forty-years-old, and I wasn't about to pretend to myself I hadn't been fucking miserable with no word from Mason. Several times, I'd picked up my phone but always found an excuse to not make a call or send a message. What was a person supposed to write or say? I'd never dated, and without anyone to ask for advice without explaining myself, I'd left it alone. Then I'd prayed the hollow feeling in my chest would ease as the days had passed with no word from Mason.

"So, you want to come on a date with me and River?" asked Mason as his eyes showed vulnerability.

A wild fluttering started in my chest and spread through me. "It seems you both already decided for me," I muttered, sounding a little churlish, but neither Mason nor River seemed to care as they gave me wide smiles.

Leaving them both grinning, I went to change into shorts. At the same time, I gave myself a talking to about getting in too deep with Mason. It was useless though, when I came down to find Mason holding a large picnic basket and River holding a blanket. There was something about the way River leaned against Mason, so trusting that he'd be there for her.

"We's got everything for our date," River announced, loud enough to make the remaining folks who sat waiting for their appointments turn to look at me, and then Mason. I scowled at the curious faces before stomping out the door.

It would be all over town before the end of the day, that I had a date with Mason. It took a second to register that I wasn't as bothered about that as maybe I should be. It was sure to get back to the club members, and as things were already tense in the clubhouse, it was hard to determine what this nugget of information would do. A part of me couldn't find it in me to care.

When I'd left Sid and gone to the club last week, there'd been more than a few shocked faces at seeing me there. It had shown me that the root of my problems possibly went deeper than I'd thought. I'd had another word with Sid, in private, and we'd considered changing our plan for Ned, Stevie, Ricky, and Doddie, but I'd contacted Dog myself and we'd decided to leave things the way they were.

"Are you's ignorin' us, Poppy?" River's breathless question forced me to stop walking and put aside my worries as I glanced down at her flushed face and heaving chest. I looked over my shoulder and, seeing how far behind me Mason was, realized how fast I'd been walking.

"Sorry, Spirit, I was just thinking 'bout something." I flicked the end of River's nose before offering a smile of apology to Mason.

This was probably not what he had in mind when he'd gone behind my back to hijack me.

"You in a rush to eat?" His expression asked something completely different. The concern wasn't quite masked as he stopped in front of me.

The buzz of the insects enjoying the flowers, and the sound of traffic, disappeared as he held my gaze. The warm scented air filled my nose as I inhaled to try and release the tight band constricting my chest. What was it about this man that made me want...more?

Choosing not to think about the obvious answer, I held out my hand. He took it without hesitation and his warm fingers interlaced mine. A part of me acknowledged how right it felt, even when another part wanted to run for the fucking hills.

River took my other hand and gave me an encouraging smile as if she understood how huge this was for me. With the three of us linked, we walked to Stillhouse Lake while River chatted.

We found a quiet spot in the shade of a tree but close enough to the water for River to paddle around. As the evening wore on, and the sun started to dip in the sky, I lay on my side on the blanket. Stuffed from the food, I sipped at my favorite beer feeling way more content than I'd ever imagined possible.

It had been a bit awkward at first when we'd all begun to eat, and we'd received several interested stares as people had passed, but Mason had ignored them and kept his focus on River and me. It was more intoxicating than the beer to be the center of all that attention. I took another deep swallow to try and wet my dry mouth.

Would he be that attentive in bed? A blind man could see we had chemistry. Fuck, we'd be able to compete with the Fourth of July fireworks, but was that all it was? Or were the warm feelings that seemed to fill my whole chest when he looked at me like there was only me, saying there could be more?

Exhaling a shaky breath, I put down the empty bottle and propped my head in my hand as my elbow rested on the ground. The dwindling sunlight haloed River and Mason at the water's edge. Her laughter floated on the evening breeze as she splashed water at Mason while he dodged her, his laughter matching hers. His face was alight with real enjoyment as they played.

A wave of grief rose up so fast, I couldn't stop the sob that got caught in my throat. Would Lizzie be proud of the way I'd raised her child? A tear slid down my cheek and I sat up and swiped at my face with the back of my hand. *Stop this shit!*

The grief couldn't be tamed as I mourned what Lizzie was missing. There was a scream before River's giggle and shouted out, "Mason you's soakin' me."

Mason swept her up into his arms, uncaring that she was drenching him, and buried his face in her neck making her laugh harder. "I think we're as wet as each other. But I know someone who isn't," he said in a stage whisper as his head lifted and he aimed a playful grin in my direction.

My heart stopped for a brief moment and the warmth was back, covering my grief in a protective cocoon. *I was so fucked!*

My Adam's apple bobbed repeatedly as Mason strode with purpose toward me, holding my child like a precious gift. How did you fight against someone who treats your baby girl like that?

Would Lizzie have loved Mason? The second the question registered through my buzzing ears, I scrambled to stand up in a panic.

No, no, it's not love.

Then what is it?

Fuck if I knew.

But love, the kind Mason would want, had no place in my life.

Whatever he read on my face, his smile dimmed for a brief moment before it came back, looking a little more forced.

"Let's get Poppy," River shouted as Mason got within reaching distance.

And they did. By the time we'd finished messing around, I was as wet as them. When River couldn't stop yawning, I called it a night and we packed up. We walked back home in companionable silence, and I didn't object when Mason took hold of my hand, linking our fingers while carrying River, who'd refused to let him go. By the time we'd gotten back to the house, she was asleep in his arms.

"I'll put her down, if you'd like?" The yearning look he wore was hard to resist, and against my better judgement, I agreed.

While Mason took River to her room, I went and changed out of my wet clothes. In just a pair of cut-offs, I went to River's room. Mason tucked the light pink blanket around River's sleeping form, his expression softening as he stroked the hair off her face before he stood up.

The earlier feelings returned, only this time I had no chance to shore up any defense when Mason faced me. His soft, loving expression touched my heart in ways that only Lizzie and River had. Breathless from the ball of emotion lodged in my throat, I stared at him.

Could I put my faith in him?

As if he'd read my mind, he came toward me and stood inches from me, his eyes daring me to try to accept him and what he freely offered.

"Do you wanna stay?"

JP Sayle

Chapter 24

Mason

Was he asking me to stay the night or just to fuck? I wasn't able to distinguish between the two, with the tension buzzing between us. "Are you asking me to spend *the night*?" I asked hesitantly.

If he only wanted a quick fuck, then I wanted to say I'd be brave enough to refuse, but I knew differently. Right then, I'd take whatever he was offering me after I'd seen the grief on his face when he'd been watching me with River. I'd somehow known he'd been thinking about his sister. His expression had torn at my heart and left me with a need to make it better for him in any way I could. To make him forget that life could be painful and replace it with something special.

He didn't answer me, but instead held out his hand. I slid mine into his and he led me out of River's room, quietly closing the door, A part of me acknowledged that this was where we'd been heading, from the moment I'd laid eyes on him.

Entering his bedroom for the first time, I glanced about the masculine room. The walls were cream, and only the one opposite the large oak-framed bed held pictures, one of River and one of Lizzie. The similarity between the two faces was striking, and I was reminded of Linc's eyes as I stared at the photos. "Your sister was beautiful," I murmured.

The heat of his body penetrated my still damp shirt as his arms enfolded me from behind. His warm breath touched my neck before his lips. "I don't wanna think about Lizzie right now."

His tone indicated I should drop the subject, so I tilted my head to the side and gave his mouth better access to my neck. I leaned back into his embrace and his arms tightened. His heart thudded against my back, and I groaned as his tongue traced a line from the crook of my neck, up to my ear. He blew on the wet skin and sent a shiver through me.

His mouth moved to my ear and he whispered, "I'm gonna fuck you till you can't remember your own name, then I'm gonna do it again."

My whole body shuddered, and a wave of dizziness swept over me as all the blood circulating in my body decided to relocate in my groin. "Promises, promises," I gasped as his teeth bit at my lobe and one of his large hands pressed against my lower stomach while he ground his hard length against my ass.

"It ain't a promise, it's a threat," he rasped in that smoky voice that did crazy things to my heart.

His arms released me, but I didn't get time to protest their loss before he took hold of the hem of my T-shirt and tugged it up over my head. I stood waiting to see what he'd do next, not daring to look back at him for fear he'd stop. I didn't need to wait long when his fingers dug into the waistband of my shorts and underwear. There was the sound of movement behind me before he slid my clothes down my bare legs. It was only when I felt his hot breath touch my ass cheek that I realized he'd knelt behind me.

The second the air touched my dick, goosebumps rode up all over my body and my fingernails dug into my palms to stop myself from stroking my throbbing flesh. Last thing I wanted to do was blow my load before we'd even started. Only thing was, he'd gotten me so worked up that I wasn't sure if I could hold back.

"Lift up," he tapped at the leg he wanted me to lift.

Concentrating on that, I lifted first one, then the other leg as he freed me from my clothes and shoes. He remained on his knees behind me as his hands stroked up my legs, till he reached my hip bones. His fingers skimmed over my skin, tiny licks of desire spreading through my body as I moaned low in my throat, very aware that River was in the next room.

Then his lips touched my ass and opened. His tongue lapped at the skin while his fingers continued to stroke over my lower abdomen, close enough to touch my cock that pulsed and bobbed to show how much it loved Linc's gentle touches.

Emotions swelled in the center of my chest, making it hard to think. Any thoughts that this would be a quick fuck disappeared as Linc paid homage to my ass with his lips and tongue. As the warm, wet tongue slid between my ass cheeks, I mewled.

His tongue teased the crease before his hands stopped their torment and moved to my ass to spread my cheeks. My knees buckled when his tongue pressed against the rim and he groaned. Hot breath gusted over my hole as he murmured against my flesh, "You taste fuckin' unbelievable."

With nothing to say to that, I locked my quivering knees and hoped like hell I didn't embarrass myself by toppling over when his tongue got busy.

I wasn't sure who was making the most noise as I struggled to keep quiet. Linc's fingers dug painfully into my ass, holding my clenching cheeks apart. My cock dripped its approval all over the wooden floor in front of me. My hips rocked back, and Linc growled as his tongue slid into my body.

"Oh fuck…shit…Linc!" I cried out, forgetting to keep quiet under the onslaught of desire flowing through me. I grabbed for my cock, panting and ringing the base to stop the impending orgasm as Linc worked a finger into my ass alongside his tongue.

He didn't let up as his tongue lapped at my sensitive skin leaving a trail of saliva he used as lube to stretch me. By the time he had three fingers in my ass, my whole body was shaking. Sweat coated my skin and I was struggling to think past the need to come on his fingers. Sheer willpower, and the need to have him inside me, kept me ringing my cock.

"Christ, I'm ready for fucksake," I ground out breathlessly.

When he finally removed his fingers and mouth from my body, I let out a relieved moan, only to find myself physically lifted and carried to the bed. I was by no means small, and the show of strength did funny things to my insides while the hungry stare that met mine left me breathless.

His careful handling of me as he laid me on the bed left my heart exposed. He stepped back and let me look my fill as he removed his cut-offs. His body was stunning. It wasn't a gym honed body, more one that showed he wasn't afraid of hard work. His broad chest was the only place that had tattoos. His thighs were thick, his cock was long and wide, and the hair at the base was dark and a little unruly.

I waxed, having always preferred smooth skin, yet, as I stared at him, I wanted to run my fingers through the silky hair to see if it was as soft as it looked. There were scars that spoke to the battles he'd endured, and it made me ache for him in a different way.

As if sensing my mood shift, he went to the bedside cabinet and retrieved lube and two condoms, one of which he threw on the bed next to me, reminding me of his earlier promise.

My ass clenched as he gloved up and used a liberal amount of lube on his cock. When he crawled over top of me, his hair fell in a shroud around us. The intimate feeling it gave left me yearning as I reached up to take hold of his cheeks.

His cock nudged at my sensitive rim. I groaned as he rocked against me and put pressure on my dick that was trapped between us. The evidence of my arousal smeared over both of us as he continued to torment me. "Please," I begged.

The air left my lungs in a rush as he thrust into me in one long stroke and his pelvis met my groin. He held still, his eyes holding me captive with dark intensity.

His cock felt as if it had hit my tonsils as I struggled to breathe through the full feeling, and the buzz of pain that accompanied it. Then his lips lowered to mine, and the pain was forgotten as his desire for me was all I could taste while he devoured my mouth.

His hips started to move slowly back and forth, his cock grazing my prostate in the most delicious way. That, with the assault on my mouth, had me moving. It seemed to give him the green light because his hips sped up and took me into a world of soul-searing pleasure that I hoped would never end.

His mouth left mine as our chests heaved in unison from the lack of oxygen.

The raw passion etched into his face as he looked at me, stole my ability to think, never mind breathe. Something passed over his face so fast I couldn't comprehend what it was before he rose up slightly and his hips started to piston so fast, I could do nothing but cling onto his bulging biceps.

As the maddening tingle in my balls licked its way down my cock and into my ass, I sucked in a noisy breath as my body let go. "Holyyyyyyyy fuckkkkkk!" I cried in a strangled whisper as hot spurts of cum fired from my body, hitting anything in its path. My cock pulsed and throbbed as Linc ground his body against mine.

My body arched up as he continued to seek his own pleasure, his face a fierce mask of concentration. That his whole focus was on me, extended my orgasm, and though the spurts were less forceful, my cock continued to release cum.

"Yessssssssss," Linc cried as he buried his face in my neck, his large body convulsing on top of mine as he found his release. His hips rocked against mine, and cum spread up my body in a sticky mess, but I didn't care as I wrapped my arms around him and held him close.

The minutes ticked by as he relaxed against me, while I stroked my hands along the length of his back, and our breathing settled.

His mouth nuzzled into the side of my neck, his whiskers brushing against the delicate skin, causing me to shiver in delight.

"You cold?" he murmured. His body shifted over mine as if trying to get closer, not that there was any space between us with him still lying fully on top of me.

"No, I'm fine," I answered, twisting my head a little to look at him.

He shifted slightly to meet my gaze, the lazy smile I was coming to love gracing his mouth. "Good, cause I've a threat to make good on." My laugh turned into a groan as his mouth met mine in a hungry kiss.

JP Sayle

Chapter 25

Lincoln

The last few weeks had flown by in a flurry of dates and unexpected trips to places I'd never bothered to visit, as Mason worked on exploring all that Belton had to offer. I'd always been so caught up in the club, work, and River, it was a surprise to realize the town that had been my home all this time had so many things to do. And Mason had made it his mission to show me.

He made it impossible for me to find my balance, to take a step back. Even when I didn't see him for a few days when work got in the way, he was all I could think about. It was fucking with my head, it had to be, when all I could think about was the next time we'd be together.

It wasn't all about the sex either, although the sex was off the charts good. No, I wanted time with him. He was funny, light-hearted, loving, giving, and created an inner peace inside me I'd never experienced with anyone. Even the grief I'd carried since Lizzie's death seemed to have lessened with his quiet presence. And it begged the question, what did he see in me?

Evidently, he didn't see the bad boy, and he didn't appear to listen to the snide comments from the townsfolks when we were out. He just clung to my fingers tighter and stood tall. All these things made it harder and harder to fight what was growing between us. Did I want more? Could someone like him really see a future with me? Why was I thinking about more when I'd never wanted it before?

He sees you. He sees the light beneath the dark.

I ran my fingers through my hair, eying the open door as I listened to the clash of music coming from downstairs and next door. Could I talk to Nutty about this? *Nah,* she was biased and had made no bones about how happy she was about the amount of time Mason spent here. Kyle, on the other hand, was still acting weird, but he might be a better option.

As if I'd somehow conjured him up, his head appeared through the open door.

"Hey, Linc, you got a sec to look at a design? Somethin' is off, but I can't figure out what it is, and the guy is due in shortly."

His face showed frustration, so I nodded and strode toward him. "I've got a few minutes before Mason gets here."

His expression immediately changed, and he grinned up at me. "He's eager that's like the fourth time he's been here in the last couple weeks, right?" Kyle's brow pinched before it smoothed out. "You're a lucky bastard. You got a real sweetheart there."

My feet faltered at the depth of feeling that came from those words. Had *I* gotten a real sweetheart? If so, what was I supposed to do about it with all that was going to go down at the weekend? "I suppose," I muttered, not sure how to respond. "He's like no man I've ever met before."

Kyle chuckled. "That's because the only guys you meet are at the clubhouse...or the hook-ups in Austin. You can't compare those to someone like Mason. That man has long-term commitment written all over him."

My throat suddenly became dry, and I struggled to swallow. A thin layer of sweat beaded my brow as I stood inside Kyle's room, feeling as if I was hurtling down the highway at one-hundred miles an hour with nothing to shield my body. I blew out a frustrated breath. "Show me the design."

I used the design as an excuse to see if I could get him to talk to me about whatever was going on with him. Twenty minutes later, the design was altered, and Kyle had remained tight-lipped. I walked down the stairs, huffing in frustration. He'd told me in no uncertain terms to butt out, so I'd shut up, because I hated when folks got into my business.

A smile formed on my lips as I hit the bottom step. The habit of waiting for Mason in the shop was something I'd sort of slipped into over the last few weeks, though I tried not to think too hard about it.

Nutty was on the phone as I hit the bottom stair. She gave me a bright smile while she carried on talking. "Yep, that's right, it will be January before there's an open appointment. Yep. I know. Cool." The conversation continued, with Nutty giving one or two word answers as she scribbled in the schedule.

When she put the phone down, she scowled. "Why do folks not get that you have a waiting list?" she complained.

I didn't get a chance to answer as Mason walked through the door, looking every bit the high-powered lawyer he was. Although his suit jacket was missing and was probably in the car, as was his habit when he drove, he still looked every inch the professional. The pale pink shirt looked a little limp from the heat, but he smelled crisp and fresh as he came toward me. His navy pants were cut to fit him perfectly, and I knew they would hug his perfect ass. An ass I worshiped and couldn't wait to get my hands on after not seeing him for the last two days.

He acknowledged Nutty with a grin, but the audience sitting and gawking in the waiting room he paid no attention to as he stepped into my body, his mouth lifting for a kiss. With the heat and scent of him surrounding me, there was no thought of refusing him.

The tug of arousal unfurled inside me, and I took hold of the nape of his neck. Our gazes met and held for a brief second. The warmth and affection swirling in Mason's sea-green eyes created a warm sensation in the center of my chest. The overwhelming feelings that followed were becoming all too familiar.

To distract myself, I kissed him. His mouth opened and there was the taste of coffee and something sweet. His tongue slid against mine and he sought to dominate. I growled low in my throat and he tugged me flush against him. I was aware that Mason liked to switch in bed. He'd said nothing so far, but the last couple of times we'd been together, he'd started to test the water by playing with my ass. Although my head seemed opposed, there were times, like now, that a part of me wanted to give up control and see what he'd do. Yet I knew if I took that step, I'd be offering more than just my ass. I'd be offering him...everything.

Conflicted and out of breath, I released his lips and dropped my hand. I barely resisted adjusting my dick as it pressed uncomfortably against my fly. There was no way the folks sitting in the seats couldn't see how aroused I was. I twisted to meet each and every person's gaze, giving them a 'what the fuck are you looking at' glare. There were several coughs and some heated faces, but no one dared to show disgust.

Mason chuckled and took my hand, his fingers intertwining with mine. "Come on, I'm starving. See you this evening, Nutty."

I didn't dissuade Mason of his assumption that Nutty would be joining us. She'd taken to spending some of her evening eating with us as her new mystery man was away on business. River was having a sleepover at Luna's, so I'd asked Nutty to keep out of our way tonight. She'd made plans to go and stay at one of her girlfriends for the night, which meant, for the very first time, we'd have the apartment to ourselves.

"You're always hungry, you need to take better care of yourself," I muttered as we headed up the stairs.

"Ahhh, you do care," he countered as his fingers tightened around mine.

We were halfway up the second flight of stairs, out of view, as I stopped and turned to face him. His brows arched and there was an air of uncertainty I was starting to recognize. Mason had a need to reaffirm that it was more than just sex between us. I felt the weight of his gaze boring into me and I sucked in a breath to give me a second to regroup.

"Yeah, I do. More than I thought I could. More than I think is wise, but fuck if I know what's wise when you look at me the way you are now."

I was unsure who moved first, but I found my back against the wall and Mason devouring my mouth with a passion that drove the temperature in the stairwell up by fifty degrees. "Fuck, I want you," he gasped against my mouth, his hands working to pull my T-shirt from the band of my jeans. Then, as if recalling where we were, he pulled back, his face flushed. "Sorry, shit. Where's River?" he asked, sounding breathless, and a lot sheepish, as he eyed the stairs leading up to my home.

Chuckling at how flustered he looked, I didn't let him go. My mouth roamed up the side of his neck above his collar. "River's out for the night," I murmured as my lips traced his beating pulse, feeling it leap as it registered what I was saying. "Nutty has plans…that leaves—"

"Oh fuckkkk," he moaned, not letting me finish as he wrenched his body from mine, his eyes wild.

A moan rumbled up my chest at the hunger he was displaying, and I went to pull him back against me. He held up his hands to ward me off. "Upstairs, now." There was a hard edge of dark arousal in his tone, and I found myself obeying as my dick throbbed in approval.

Chapter 26

Mason

Linc seemed to have understood that if we touched again, I wouldn't be held responsible for what happened, so he kept his distance as he moved to walk in front of me. His low-slung jeans sculpted to his ass and my fingers tingled with thoughts of being able to touch. My chest heaved with the effort to keep control of the need tearing at my insides.

The pressure inside my chest felt immense as we silently walked up the last flight of stairs and Linc opened the door into his apartment. This was the first time we'd be alone together with no possible interruption and my blood sang with anticipation.

He stood back to let me past. The cool air inside the hallway did little to calm my overheated skin. The snick of the lock engaging was all it took to break the chain on my control, and I whirled to face him. "I want you," I growled through clenched teeth. "I want to fuck you up against that wall. You gonna let me?"

His large body shuddered, and a red hue rode over his cheek bones. I held my breath as his eyes hooded. Then he took hold of the hem of his T-shirt and stripped it off. Next came his boots, socks, jeans, and lastly, his boxer briefs.

He stood aroused and unashamed, his eyes locked with mine. His dick bobbed, the tip slick and gleaming with pre-cum, and my mouth watered for a taste. I held back though, because that was not what I wanted right now. I wanted so much more, I wanted his submission. No, I yearned for it.

The last few times we'd been together, I'd held back from voicing what I really wanted. With the knowledge we were completely alone, it had somehow broken through the barrier that had stopped me before.

"You want me"—his arms lifted out from his sides as if he was issuing a threat—"then take me," he rasped sexily.

My lips tugged into a smile as a buzzing started in my ears. I slowly lifted my trembling fingers to remove my tie, then unbutton my shirt. His eyes darkened as my chest was revealed. I unbuttoned the cuffs then let the shirt drop to the floor next to my tie. With my shoes and socks off, I peeled off my pants.

I dug into my pocket to pull out my wallet, retrieving a condom and a packet of lube, placing them on the small table within reach. Only then did I push my boxer briefs down my thighs and step out of them.

My skin felt electrified by the tension crackling between us. His hungry gaze raked my body, and my cock bucked to show its appreciation. I stroked my dick from base to tip. His lips thinned as his jaw bunched when I did it several more times before collecting the pre-cum beaded on the slit.

His nostrils flared as I stepped to him, my intention clear as I lifted my slick finger and smeared his lips with pre-cum. His mouth opened, but before his tongue could taste, I surged forward and bodily pushed him back against the wall near the table.

He growled, his eyes dark pools of desire as I took his mouth in a wet, hungry kiss. The salty taste of my pre-cum combined with his unique flavor was all I could think about as his tongue slid deep into my mouth. One hand took hold of the back of my neck while the other roamed down my back. His fingers dug painfully into my buttock as his hips thrust forward. His dick slid against mine in a sensual caress that was too much, and yet, not nearly enough.

Aware that Linc was trying to take back control, I peeled my lips away from his reluctantly. When his mouth chased mine, my heart soared. "Who's in charge?" The hard edge I added to my voice got Linc's attention and his eyes became dark pools of lust while the large body I was pressed against, tensed. There were so many emotions riding over his face, I couldn't keep up. Would he let me take control?

As if I'd voiced that aloud, his body went lax against the wall and his hands dropped to his sides. His eyes were wary, but he didn't look away as I inched closer to his mouth. My lips hovered over his, "Thank you. I swear, you can trust me."

He shifted and his breathing rate increased. "You gonna fuck me or just talk 'bout it?"

It was the uncertainty I could hear that stopped me from saying more. Instead, I traced my tongue over his lower lip. His breath mingled with mine and he moaned, his dick pulsing against my lower body. "No, I'm gonna love on that ass of yours until"—I sucked his lower lip into my mouth and bit gently—"I make you my bitch."

His whole body shuddered, and I slammed my mouth against his. He grunted and opened to let me take control of the kiss. The kiss was hot, demanding, and hard, as teeth clashed together, and my tongue tasted every part of his mouth. Using my body to pin him to the wall, my hips rolled against Linc's. My satiny skin sliding against his silky hair added to my torment. There were moans and groans, but I wasn't sure who they belonged to as my hands roamed freely over the large body that was *all mine*. This glorious man was mine to cherish. How had I gotten so lucky?

My mouth traveled down Linc's throat, his extra height making it easier. His body was a thing of beauty, and I wanted to worship every inch of him. Aware of the off-limits part of his chest, I lifted my left hand and stroked his nipple while I licked a path to the other side of his chest, the dark, firm bud calling to me. I sucked it into my mouth and lavished it with attention, then I bit hard while squeezing the other, knowing Linc loved a little pain.

"Oh, fuck yeah," he rasped huskily. His pelvis thrust hard against mine, his slick dick giving mine a wet kiss as they slid together in a sticky caress. My dick throbbed and my balls got a nice ache, reminding me that I needed to get things moving along if I wanted to give Linc the little piece of heaven I'd promised.

I reached out blindly for the table I'd placed the lube and condom on. There was a crash before it registered something had been knocked off the table.

"Fuck," I gasped, dragging in a ragged breath as I glanced at the now broken lamp. "Sorry, I'll replace it."

"Fuck the lamp," he groaned, his hands moving impatiently at his sides, his eyes demanding I get on with it.

I was sure the strain on his face matched my own. Raw need ravaged me as the desire to show Linc how I really felt about him, even if it was only with my body, took hold. There were barriers that he'd erected to keep himself safe from pain, from suffering at the hands of others' carelessness, I could see them. They were there in the depths of his gaze and I wanted to prove to him that this meant everything to me. That *he* meant everything to me.

My fingers shook as I ripped open the condom and made quick work of gloving up. The throbbing ache made it difficult to touch myself with Linc watching my every move. Opening the packet of lube, I slicked up my fingers and my cock before I stepped closer to Linc.

Puffs of warm air hit my face as Linc's eyes closed when I cupped his heavy sac, rolling his hairy balls in the palm of my hand. Using my other slicked hand, I teased the slit of his cock. His eyes remained shut as he groaned and pushed into my hand, his body begging me for more.

Ever watchful, I continued to tease his dick as I slid my other hand under his sac and pressed against his taint. His lips clamped together, and a deep flush rode high on his cheek bones. He widened his stance and his hips tilted forward to give me better access, even though his eyes remained closed.

My jaw ached. The heat and scent of him surrounded me as my finger slid between his ass cheeks and stroked over his tightly clenched hole. His chest sawed, and deep lines appeared at the side of his mouth, but he uttered no protest.

"God, look at you. You look so fucking sexy standing there with my hands touching you. Can you feel my fingers trembling with need for you?" As I spoke, he shivered and mewled but his eyes stayed shut, and that wasn't working for me. I wanted him to see who it was that was touching him, pleasuring him. "Look at me," I growled.

It took a second, but his eyes slitted open. They glittered with wild desire and my heart skipped several beats. I leaned forward and took his mouth in a hungry kiss, using it to distract him from what my hands were doing. I deepened the kiss until his hands came up to cup the back of my head to hold me in place.

A growl of lust rumbled up my chest as my finger pressed a little more firmly against him. He tensed, but as I was about to retreat, he bore down, and I murmured encouragement into his mouth as I slipped my finger into the tightest ass I'd ever encountered.

He panted into my mouth as his ass clenched and unclenched several times.

"Relax Linc, the burning will fade, and it'll feel so good, I swear."

Sweat covered his forehead as he worked on doing as I suggested. Once the clenching muscles released my finger enough that I could move it, I felt for his prostate. The second I hit pay dirt and stroked gently, his whole body bucked hard enough to nearly dislodge me.

"Motherfucker…do that again," he cried out on a strangled moan.

"What, this?" I asked as I got busy making his ass sing with pleasure.

"Yes, fucker!" he growled before his head landed hard against the wall. He seemed not to notice as I slowly pumped my finger into his ass, making sure to stroke his prostate. His dick thickened and pulsed in my other hand, reminding me of what I'd been doing. I stroked it in time with the shallow pumps into his ass and only when he begged for more, did I add a second finger.

Linc's hair was stuck to his shoulders and his face was sheened with sweat by the time I had three fingers in his ass, and he was humping my hand for all he was worth. This time his eyes remained open and heavy lidded. His lips were parted as he cursed, moaned, and groaned his pleasure for me to hear. His desire was like an aphrodisiac that stoked my own need higher and higher.

"Fuck me, fuck me now, you bastard. Do it now. Stop fucking teasing me," he demanded, sounding strained and angry.

Hoping that I'd done enough, I removed my fingers from his slick hole and pressed my body flush against his. Our chests slid against each other as I nestled my pelvis in the crook of his and nudged the tip of my dick against his hole. "Are you ready to be my bitch?" I ground out through clenched teeth.

There was acceptance and vulnerability in the depth of his gaze as it held mine. "Do it," he whispered.

Whatever I'd thought I felt for this man was surpassed in the moment of absolute truth and honesty, as we continued to stare at each other. Nothing else mattered but this right here...the love I felt for him and was coming to understand was as vital to me as breathing. I blinked back the tears gathering at the corner of my eyes and tightened my hold, fighting the fear that I might not be enough.

I pushed into him and the air left my lungs in a rush. The heat and tight muscles cinching my dick as I inched into heaven left me struggling to recall my moves. "Fuck, you're so fucking tight," I gasped, working to suck in some air.

"That's 'cause you're trying to shove a pole into a fuckin' pin hole," he grunted breathlessly, his face looking more than a little pinched when my groin met his.

Humor replaced the fear as I struggled to keep from laughing at his answer, knowing that he needed to relax his ass. That he had to be feeling the burn right then with the way his channel was squeezing the fuck out of my dick.

Chapter 27

Lincoln

Breathe, breathe, I chanted, hoping it would help with the unfamiliar sensations running wildly through me. The fullness and burning in my ass were a part of it, but that wasn't what was causing my panic. No, it was the feelings of rightness the moment Mason had pushed inside me. Expecting to feel emasculated, I'd never felt more powerful in my fucking life.

Mason's face was a myriad of emotions he wasn't concealing and that overtook my common sense. I'd swear it was that as I reached out for his hand and took hold of his wrist. His eyes showed some confusion until I brought the palm of his hand to my lips and kissed it. With wide eyes sheened with moisture, his lips trembled when I laid his hand on my chest and pressed it tightly over my beating heart. A heart this man had slowly been claiming, piece by piece, since he'd stepped into my life.

"Oh fuck...I know you're not ready for the words, but know that when you're ready, they're yours." His fingers traced Lizzie's tattoo as his eyes offered me everything. "I'll treasure what you've given me." He voice was no more than a broken whisper before he gently kissed me.

Certain the dreamy sigh I heard came from him, I deepened the kiss, my ass forgotten as Mason reverently stroked the skin over my heart. I might not be able to say how I felt, but it seemed Mason had gotten the meaning behind my gesture. The kiss was endless and gave my ass time to realize it was ready for whatever Mason had planned. Refusing to release his mouth, I rocked my hips forward and groaned when the angle allowed his dick to press against my prostate.

Mason followed my lead and slowly eased out, before pushing back in. He kept his rhythm slow and steady. It was maddening. It wasn't nearly enough. "Faster, fuck me harder. I won't fucking break." I bit his lower lip to make my point. "I thought you said you were gonna make me your bitch?" I added several fast hips thrusts to show him I wasn't made of glass.

Stormy eyes immobilized me as Mason inched back, his gaze searching my face. Whatever he found there seemed to satisfy him. Next thing I knew, his hands slid up under my armpits and his fingers moved up to grip the top of my shoulders in a punishing hold.

His smile was feral as he snarled, "Yes, I did." His dick tunneled into my body and lit up my ass as he pulled my body down hard against him. He was unrelenting as skin slapped against skin, sounding like someone was getting a violent beating. There was no finesse as he fucked me into the wall, and I loved it.

His eyes remained on me, claiming me as he'd promised. His jaw bunched and sweat slid down his face, but he didn't stop. Cum bubbled in my sac as his sweat-slicked skin slid against mine and my arousal rubbed against his rippling abs. His hips started to falter, and his fingers dug into my shoulders as he tilted his pelvis, ramming his hips at an angle that hit my prostate head on. At the same time, he used his lower body to rub against my dick, and it was game over.

"Massssssssoooonnnnn," I cried in ecstasy, as my vision blurred and my whole body burned with sensations that fried my brain until all there was nothing but pleasure.

My head thudded against the wall as my legs struggled to hold me upright and warmth filled my ass. I groaned, rejoicing that Mason had found his own release inside me. The weight of his body pressed me into the wall as he collapsed against me. Hot puffs of breath hit my skin, and little aftershocks of pleasure rippled through me as he wrapped his arms around me.

With him cocooning me, it took a while for my pleasure fired brain to register how safe and protected I felt. The simple gesture meant more to my battered and scarred heart than any words. My heart leapt against my ribs, and I struggled to slow my breathing.

As if sensing my inner turmoil, Mason stroked at my arms while his cheek came to rest on my damp shoulder.

"Give me a sec till the feeling comes back in my legs, and I'll move," he muttered.

Needing a distraction from all the emotions that he caused, I replied, "You're not up for round two, then?"

His head slowly rose, and what I saw in the depth of his gaze did little to help with my gaining a semblance of control.

Mason's lips peeled back from his teeth as he gave me a toothy grin. "Oh, you want more?" His mouth nuzzled into my damp hair, right before his teeth sunk into the junction of my neck and shoulder, causing me to groan. His hips shifted and his semi hard cock jabbed at my sensitive prostate. "Let's take this to the bedroom."

I gritted my teeth as his cock slipped out of my aching ass, and for a moment I considered if I might have been too hasty asking for another round. Then a smug smile formed on Mason's face and I found myself saying, "Bring it."

Saturday morning, as I shifted on the seat of my hog, my ass twinged and reminded me never to utter the words 'bring it' to Mason ever again. The man was a fucking machine when he got started. He'd turned me inside out as he'd fucked me not only in the hallway and bedroom, but over the kitchen table when we'd decided to get out of bed and eat something.

A shiver of desire raced down my spine, and my ass clenched in anticipation. I was loathed to admit it, but the fucker had turned me into his bitch far too easily for my liking. Heat filled my face as I recalled how I begged him for more. If the guys at the club found out, I'd never live it down.

The activity around me, and the throb of the engine under me, gave me something else to think about. I looked to Sid and gave him a nod before signaling to everyone that it was time to hit the road. Slipping my sunglasses on, I secured my open-faced helmet and inhaled a deep earthy breath, working to clear the dregs of tiredness from my brain.

The storm the night before had cleared the air and the sun was just tickling the horizon over the trees surrounding the clubhouse. It was barely six o'clock in the morning, and the sound of engines reving filled the silence.

We'd planned an early ride to avoid the heat of the day and prevent us from melting in our leathers. I'd opted for wearing jeans with my leather jacket. The large patch over my back, with the word, Killer, and the club emblem above, identified who I was.

As I took off and roared down the dirt road, all that could be heard behind me was the sound of motorcycles. The usual buzz I got from one of these planned rides was absent when all I could think about what would come next. What it could mean to the future I was starting to envision with Mason.

I sighed into the wind as it brushed over my face. When he'd left me yesterday morning to go home and get changed for work, I'd said goodbye with mixed emotions. With plans that didn't include him in my weekend, it had left a sour taste in my mouth I didn't like.

Up till now, I'd kept the club and him completely separate. I didn't talk about it in front of him and shut him down when he asked any questions that could lead to me revealing anything that could touch him professionally. I was more than aware that having a relationship with me could create waves in his law practice.

So, I'd brushed off his suggestion that he come with me this weekend and get to know the men in the club. The offer left me stunned, but the reality of what this weekend was all about sat between us, whether he knew it or not. I wasn't sure if he sensed I was holding back, but plans had been set in motion and, as I was president, I couldn't back down, regardless of how shitty it left me feeling when Mason had tried and failed miserably to hide his disappointment at my refusal of his offer.

I squeezed the accelerator, increasing my speed and hoping to outrun the face filling my head as I hit the highway. Deal with the club issues first, then think about what happens next with Mason.

What if the club issues are what happens next with Mason? My shoulders tensed. The club comes first, it always has.

Does it mean that it always has to?

JP Sayle

Chapter 28

Mason

I roamed around my apartment, feeling at loose ends with no extra work to occupy my time and no Linc or River to have fun with. I was miffed that Linc had refused my offer to go with him this weekend. And okay, I wasn't all that keen on getting on the back of his big ass motorcycle, but I'd offered like a good boyfriend should.

Recalling the impenetrable mask his face had become, my stomach knotted unpleasantly. I had a feeling this weekend away up in Austin was about more than just a ride. But Linc was locked down tighter than Fort Knox when it came to talking about the club or club business.

When I'd mentioned taking out a suit against Miss Fink, after her continued bad mouthing of Linc to anyone who'd listen, he'd shut me down. It was frustrating as fuck, when all I wanted to do was help him, protect him. I understood that he'd never had anyone offer that kind of support, except maybe the club members, but I needed him to see he could trust me.

The palm of the hand he'd kissed, then laid against his chest, tingled, and warmth spread through me. *He does trust me.* That action showed me how much, after what he'd mentioned when I'd first touched his chest without thought. Then why didn't he want me to go with him this weekend?

I threw up my arms in frustration and went to find my phone to see if Luis was going to the gym. I needed to burn off some of this excess energy that wouldn't let me settle. If I couldn't be with Linc and River, then my older brother was my next best option.

"Yo, what are you ringing me for on a Saturday morning?" Luis answered on the second ring, sounding far too chirper.

"I'm at loose ends and wanted to know if you're training today?"

"Is the Pope Catholic? Of course, I'm going to the gym." He chuckled, and there was the sound of rasping like he was brushing at his whiskers.

"Want a buddy?"

"What's up? I'd have thought you'd be hanging with Linc now that the two of you are an item. I didn't get that wrong, did I? It sure looked like there was something between the two of you the last time I saw you both at Mom and Dad's."

"We are, I think." I groaned at how pathetic I sounded.

"Oh, right...okay. Meet me at the gym in thirty, and we can talk then."

With that, Luis ended the call and I went to change into some gym gear before heading out with my sports bag slung over my shoulder. In the car, I opened the windows to try and dispel some of the heat as I eyed the cloudless blue sky. I swallowed a sigh and slipped my sunglasses on to stop the from sun blinding me. Blasting out Carrie Underwood, I pulled out of my parking space and drove down the street with the hope a couple of hours in the gym would release the knots in my stomach.

At the gym, I stored my sports bag in the locker they'd allocated to me and walked out of the locker room to find my brother.

What the hell had compelled me to believe this was a good idea?

Two hours later, I gasped for air. The muscles in my legs screamed at me to stop torturing them as Luis, the bastard, made me pay for my stupidity. The quivering in my thighs increased as I pressed my feet flat to the plate and pushed up until my knees locked out.

"That's it. Remember to squeeze your abdominal muscles to protect your lower back," he reminded me.

"How the fuck do you squeeze something that feels like a noodle?" I ground out through my gritted teeth as I tried to do as he suggested.

"Remember, you wanted to come and train with me." he fired back with an evil grin on his face.

The second the metal clanged, and the weight released off my legs. I let go of the grab bars at my sides and used an arm to swipe at my forehead before more sweat could sting my eyes. "I said workout, not, kill me," I panted, not at all ashamed I was completely out of breath. We'd been at this for two very long hours. There wasn't a part of me that didn't know it.

I twisted and grunted as I sat up on the edge of the leg press. "You're a sadist, you know that?"

His brows waggled at me as he glanced over to the guy using the shoulder press. "You think I'm a sadist, Peters?"

The guy didn't look in our direction when he answered, "Yep. That's why your body looks like that and the rest of us mere mortals can only dream about looking as good as you."

Hoping my legs would hold me, I got up, clutching at the bench press and laughing at Luis's bewildered expression. "You do have a mirror, right?"

His face pinked with what looked like embarrassment before he glanced away. Letting it slide, because right then all I wanted was a hot shower and some food, I limped off toward the locker room.

I'd gotten only a couple of steps before Luis shouted, "Where do you think you're going? We haven't finished."

I glanced over my shoulder and widened my eyes in horror for effect. "Not finished. I think you'll find that I was finished about an hour ago. Now, I'm going to limp into the shower and pray I've enough energy to go home, lay on my couch, eat junk food, and binge watch some crap on Netflix."

He rolled his eyes at me, and I shook my head before heading to grab a shower. By the time I'd exited the gym and bought enough groceries to see me through the weekend, I'd have willingly begged someone to carry me up to my apartment.

I spent the rest of the day cursing my brother while trying not to move. Every muscle in my body felt like it'd been put in the dryer on full heat and had come out half the size and refusing to stretch back.

Late the following morning, when I finally woke after a fitful night's sleep, I'd somehow forgotten what Luis had done to me. I cursed when I couldn't figure out what hurt the most as I shifted over the mattress to the edge of the bed. It was a close call between my thighs and my triceps. Both were in agreement that the next time I had a harebrained idea to get Luis to distract me with a workout, I was to sign myself into the hospital because I clearly wasn't in my right mind.

I managed to get to the bathroom to pee, but only after I'd furniture walked around my bedroom. It was humiliating, and I was thankful that Linc wasn't there to witness my shame. Then I remembered that it was his fault. If he'd let me go with him, then I wouldn't be in this mess.

Once I managed to get back to the bed, I relaxed back against the headboard and picked up my phone. The second I opened it, a message flashed up from a number I didn't recognize. My heart thumped against my ribs as I opened the message with trembling fingers and read.

SOS! Come to this address and say nothing to no one!

After a quick search, I found where the place was outide Austin. Some instinct told me this was not someone messing with me, so I gingerly got up and dressed. It took twice as long as usual with my body rebelling at the activity.

By the time I'd gotten to my car, there was a tight band around my chest stopping me from taking a decent breath. Had something happened to Linc? Had he gotten himself into more trouble? Had he taken matters into his own hands? It was the last question that worried me the most. Linc's refusal to talk about the whole situation once the case had been thrown out of court, left me trying not to think too hard on the whys and whatfores, and if it had been some sort of setup.

There'd been a lot of documented issues with rival bike clubs over the years, and there was evidently no love lost between Linc and other clubs. Yet I suspected that maybe what had happened began closer to home. And if I were honest, it was why I'd been feeling antsy since Linc informed me he'd be going away this weekend. He wasn't a man to let folks double cross him and then walk away, without there being any retribution.

Thoughts circled around my head as I drove faster than the speed limit, with my need to make sure Linc was alright. I wasn't sure what I'd do if he wasn't.

Stop jumping the gun. If Linc needs you, then you need to be clear headed.

I clutched at my steering wheel, keeping my gaze on the asphalt while I worked to breathe through the panic that maybe this time, I wouldn't be able to help, to save him.

Chapter 29

Lincoln

We'd arrived mid-morning on the outskirts of Round Rock, the day before. Dog and his men had been there to greet us at the large cabin we'd rented for the weekend. It wasn't unlike the clubhouse, huge and made of logs, sat deep in the woods, and off the beaten track. I was told it was used for retreats and such. It had enough beds to sleep twenty people, seventeen less than we needed, but it was normal for folks to just crash wherever they fell after drinking their body weight in liquor.

This trip had started like they all did, with a huge barbecue and more alcohol than a bar, being consumed as club members let rip. These get-togethers, away from respective partners, were all about partying hard. As one of the few clubs that allowed women to claim a patch, these weekends could be unpredictable to say the least.

I'd heard that there'd been talk, after my Granddaddy had died, to ban women from obtaining membership. At the time, Swifty had been married to one of the club whores, and that put a stop to that. So, used to the club always having female members, a few with bigger balls than some men, I'd left it as it was. Then Nutty had come along. She'd fought hard to gain her patch, and with it, my respect. When River had been born, and Nutty had stepped into to help, I'd never have contemplated changing things.

I'd spoken to Nutty about this weekend, and she'd chosen to stay home and look after River. It was the only time I left River, and this time I was glad Nutty opted to keep out of what was about to go down. The storm had been brewing last night while I'd waited to see if the traitors would show themselves. Tensions had mounted between some of the men, but it appeared they, like me, had their own agendas.

With my face schooled to reveal none of what I was thinking, I entered the large room, my gaze landing on Nola, sitting on Ned's lap. My lip curled up as he stroked her bare thigh and revulsion caused bile to burn the back of my throat. The betrayal was so huge, I had to clamp my jaw tight to stop myself showing the rage that wanted to savage the bold-faced fucking traitor. Although I'd known Ned had been working to undermine my authority, it was a different thing to come face to face with it.

Sid had come to find me only minutes earlier to inform me that Nola had appeared and caused a stir. He'd barely kept hold of his temper as I'd dressed for battle. I wore a tank top with the club emblem on the front and my name on the back. It showed off my tattooed arms and the sheath strapped to my arm, holding my favored blade. There was no mistaking that I meant business, and silence descended around the room.

What had I done to deserve this treachery?

With no obvious answer, I shook off what couldn't be changed. It didn't matter why they'd targeted me, only that they had. To bring Nola here was a declaration of war and showed how far things had spiraled out of control.

The betrayal was locked down for now as I continued to move deeper into the lion's den. The sound of my boots and Sid's thudding against the wood was the only noise in the house. We stopped in the middle of the large, open-plan room, Sid remaining at my back, his own blade on display, tucked into the waistband of his leathers.

The weight of the sheath strapped to my wrist was comforting and my fingers twitched in anticipation. I carefully moved my gaze to meet the stare of every person in the room, searching to see who was with me and who wasn't.

There seemed to be a split between the old timers and the prospects, with one exception, Beau. He'd clearly opted for the wrong side, and the way he fidgeted on the leather chair he'd sprawled out on said he knew it, too.

When Dog had left the day before, there had been no mention of his return this morning, so when the sound of motorcycles cut through the silence, several faces lost their color at what that meant. There was the heavy clatter of booted feet, followed by the front door opening and ten men entering the room. Dog and Rattlesnake led the way.

There were several murmurs as Dog came and stood on my left side, opposite Sid. Only then did I focus my gaze on Ned.

"Why?" I rasped, through a throat that was parched.

There was a collective gasp from half of the room as men and women turned their attention to Ned, but no one uttered a word, understanding whatever this was, it was between me and Ned.

Nola, the stupid bitch, got off Ned's knee and faced off with me, giving me an ugly sneer. "Dirty fucking fag—" She got no further as one of the women closest to her, Tina, got up and punched her in the face. The sound of bone grinding on bone was followed by blood spurting out of Nola's nose. It fountained over her hands as she cried out. But no one, not even Ned, came to her rescue as Tina took hold of her by the hair and dragged her kicking and screaming toward Dog's men.

Tina threw Nola on the ground and spat on her. She glanced at Dog. "She wants to be a club whore, I'm sure you'll have space for her."

I felt no sense of remorse as one of Dog's men came forward and hauled Nola up. He threw her over his shoulder like she weighed nothing. Her body flopped as her head bounced off the guy's broad back, smearing blood over his leather. The last thing I heard of them was the guy slapping her wriggling ass none too gently as the door closed behind him.

The silence returned as I focused back on Ned. "You need a whore to speak for you?" I growled, taking a threatening step closer to him.

"You think I'm frightened of a pansy who likes to take it up the ass," he spat out, his voice full of venom.

I felt Sid shift at my side, and I lifted my hand to still him while I held Ned's gaze. "We're gonna find out," I threatened.

The tension rolling off certain club members increased, so I relaxed my stance, resigned to this fight. A small part of me mourned, since these men and women had been my family, my place of safety. Now they were my enemy because…of who I chose to fuck? It had to be more than that, surely? They'd always known I was gay.

There was no time to find an answer when Doddie, Stevie, and Ricky moved together to surround me, while Beau pulled out a gun and pointed it directly at me.

An angry growl came from my right, but I paid Sid no attention, my eyes remaining on the gun. I let my body sag as if in defeat, but the second I registered Beau's triumphant grin as he glanced at Ned, I flicked my wrist to release the catch holding my blade. It whistled through the air, hitting its target.

"Argh, you fuckerrrrr," Beau screamed as the gun clattered to the floor and his brother, Ram, quickly picked it up and shoved into the back of his leathers. His face was a grim mask as he watched Beau grab at the arm that had my knife embedded in it. Blood trickled down onto the wooden floor, but I had no time to think about the mess as Doddie attempted to sucker punch me.

All hell broke loose as I spun on my heel and blocked the hit. The sounds of grunts, swearing, and shouts filled the cabin as those still loyal to me fought with the traitors, but my focus was on the ring leaders. I slammed my fist into Doddie's face, catching him on the temple and busting his eyebrow open. He staggered back blindly as blood ran down into his eye and he fell.

The second he fell, hands grabbed at my T-shirt and I shifted my attention to Stevie. He had a rep of being a dirty fighter and I wasn't surprised by the gleam of steel that came toward my face. "Rat bastard," I growled as he slashed air, rather than my face, as I shifted.

I dodged his next attack and used my height to keep out of reach of the lethal knife. The thin blade could slice muscle from bone, and I'd prefer mine left where it was. I pivoted to the left and as he came at me, I lifted my booted foot to kick high, right up into his arm pit. He screamed, and the force propelled him into two men fighting behind him. The knife he held, dropped from his lifeless arm, and I hoped I'd caused enough damage to the nerves that ran under his arm that he'd never be able to use it again.

When both Ricky and Ned approached me with more caution, I had time to suck in several deep breaths to settle my racing heart. "Is this really 'cause I'm gay?" I ground out, needing to know.

"You fuckin' changed things that didn't need changin'. Your Granddaddy and Swifty proved their leadership, proved we were a club no fucker messed with. What did you do? You made us look weak by bringin' your sister's bastard child into the club. She'd have been better off buried in a box with your no-good sister,'" Ned ranted, his face a hateful mask of spite as spit ran down his chin.

White hot rage at him disrespecting my sister and the one amazing thing Lizzie had left me, River, tore at my sanity. There was no finesse as I charged at both men, fists flying. I didn't feel anything other than the burning fury that flowed like boiling hot lava out of a volcano as it crushed everything in its path until all that was left were decimated remains.

Chapter 30

Mason

The lack of sirens and flashing lights didn't ease the gut-wrenching fear from all the scenarios I'd gone through by the time I'd reached the address I'd been given. There were motorcycles everywhere I looked as I pulled up and abandoned my car as close to the cabin as I could.

I'd come to recognize some of the motorcycles from my visits to the club, but there were at least twenty I'd not seen before.

My hands trembled at my sides. Was this a set up? Was I about to get my ass kicked?

Fuck knows, just get inside and see what's what.

I was halfway up the stairs leading to the door when it opened to reveal Sid. My stomach twisted into painful knots at the bruised and battered face looking at me with worried eyes. His T-shirt was torn and covered in blood. His jeans weren't in any better shape.

"What happened? Please tell me Linc's okay." My voice cracked, and I had to stop before the tears burning the back of my eyes made good on the threat to slide down my cheeks.

Sid looked over my shoulder before answering. "He's not great. I can't seem to get through to him. He's never been like this before, not since…anyway, you were a last resort. It's why I messaged you."

What he said made little sense, but I didn't argue as he stepped aside and beckoned me in. My heart sank at the sight of carnage. There were men and women scattered around the room, not looking much better than Sid. There was broken furniture, blood splattered over many of the surfaces and some of the walls, leaving me wondering if there'd been a death.

My blood ran cold when I caught sight of a bloodied and battered man lying unmoving on the floor in the middle of the room. The face was unrecognizable, but the T-shirt he wore identified him as Ned. My heart thundered against my ribs as I narrowed my eyes on him.

Was his chest moving? Please god, don't let him be dead. Something told me that whatever had happened to Ned, it was at Linc's hands.

Air hissed past my teeth when one of his hands moved. *Thank fuck!*

Why weren't they helping him? My gaze swept the quiet room. Some of the faces I'd come to know looked belligerent and gave off warnings I'd be ill advised not to heed. Whatever had gone down, no one was going to talk to me about it and, judging by their body language, they didn't want me there.

I swore under my breath. Why had Sid messaged me? *Linc needs you.*

I searched the room for the man in question. He was standing at the back of the room, staring out a large window. The unusual stiffness of his posture screamed 'keep the fuck away.'

Leading with my heart, I shoved aside the worries my head wanted to focus on and crossed the room, though my legs wanted to rebel. I clenched my teeth together to keep the complaint to myself, not wanting to show any sign of weakness. Skirting Ned, I chose not to look down at him.

The hands balled into fists at Linc's sides, were swollen and discolored, doing little to help my rising panic. Then one of Linc's men grabbed hold of my arm, halting my progress across the room.

"Get the fuck off me," I ground out, shoving the man away, needing to get to Linc. There seemed to be a pause as everyone stared at me warily with one exception, Linc. He showed no sign that he was aware of my presence, I glanced at Sid.

He shrugged before his head nodded at me, as if encouraging me to do something.

"Linc, look at me." I demanded in a firmer tone. Still nothing, he didn't move. It was like he'd become a stone statue. With my pulse playing, let's see how many times it can leap in a minute, I closed the gap and moved to stand in front of him.

I winced at the dark stains covering his T-shirt. The smell of copper and sweat turned my stomach. But it was the vacant look in his eyes that left me struggling to breathe, so I gently touched his arm, hoping to get him to focus on me.

If it was possible, he became even stiffer. Long seconds passed, as I stroked my hands up his arms and made soothing noises. I kept my full attention on Linc, even as I felt every pair of eyes in the room on us. "Linc, sweetheart, you need to look at me. Come on, I need you to hear me," I whispered, until he blinked several times as if clearing his vision.

My breath whistled through my teeth when the blank expression was exchanged for despair that seemed engraved into the depths of his soul. It showed wounds that went far deeper than I could grasp the true meaning of. They slashed at my heart. The love I felt for him rose in a tidal wave and took charge of my actions. I cupped his cheeks and laid a gentle kiss on his lips. "Whatever happened, I'm here for you." I put as much conviction as I could into the words, even when a part of me worried it might not be enough.

His chest heaved and a shudder wracked his body. Emotions moved too fast for me to read them as they played over his face. I held my breath as the seconds ticked by and he remained silent.

Then his face became an indecipherable mask and he took a step back, so my hands fell away from him. They dropped to my sides and breathtaking pain filled my chest, but I remained still. I wanted to beg him to let me in, to tell me what he needed, but the wall that seemed to materialize between us kept me silent.

I watched him warily, to see what he'd do next, when he turned around. I moved so I could see his face, then wished I hadn't when his expression filled with hatred as he asked, "Is he dead?"

A shiver raced down my spine in the warm room and chilled me to the bone.

Sid didn't move or seek to clarify who 'he' was, instead, he shook his head. "He's pretty broken, and most likely never gonna be the same again. Dog has arranged for another wagon to pick him up and drop him at the hospital." There was no remorse as he spoke, and it struck me that this was the world that Linc was a part of. A world where those who betrayed the club would have to suffer the full force of club retribution.

My greatest fears were laid bare. Could I put aside this reality for love? There was no easy answer as I stared at Linc's unrepentant face. Was there anything that could justify this kind of violence? I wasn't sure, but with more questions than answers, I struggled to see how Ned deserved to be beaten beyond recognition.

As I tried to process it all, it took a moment to register Sid had said "another wagon." Who had gone in the first one and were they worse than Ned? Fuck. What the hell had happened here?

I again looked about the room, only then realizing that Doddie, Stevie, and Riley were missing, as were a few other men I'd interviewed in the clubhouse.

While my whole body thrummed with nervous energy, the room started to clear as if by silent agreement. Only once everyone but Linc, Sid, two men I didn't know, and Ned were gone, did I speak again. "Do I need to do some damage control?" I rasped past my dry throat as I looked at Ned then back at Linc. "Will he talk? Do I need to find you a good lawyer—"

"I have one," he stated as he glanced at me, his brow furrowing. For the first time since I'd arrived, I felt he was seeing me clearly.

"Linc, I can't defend you now." His face darkened, and he looked about ready to start arguing with me. "How the fuck can I defend you when we're in a relationship and I love you?" I ground out in frustration.

He stilled, and it dawned too late what I'd said.

Fuck, fuck, fuck!

Sid coughed, and the other two men's feet shuffled against the floor as everyone looked anywhere but at me and Linc. The strain in the room seemed to increase after I'd opened my big mouth, even though there so few of us. Why did I have to announce it like that? I ran my hands through my hair when Linc looked at me with an unreadable expression before he glanced at the other men.

"We need a cleaning crew to clean the place up," Linc said.

"All arranged. The crew I use will keep their mouths shut and I've made a list of things that need to be replaced," the bigger of the two men answered.

Linc gave a curt nod. "I'll cover the costs. The keys don't need to be returned until tomorrow evening. Will your guys have it taken care of by then?"

The casual way they carried on the conversation left my emotions in turmoil. Linc continued to act like I wasn't standing more than a couple of feet from him, or that there wasn't a man lying unconscious on the floor, potentially dying.

I glanced at Sid and wondered if his intention was to bring me here to show me what Linc was really like. The loving father and hardworking businessman was now a cold, heartless bastard. Which was the real Linc?

All of them, and deep down you knew this.

The reality was harder to acknowledge with Linc's behavior toward me adding to my inner conflict.

What the fuck was I going to do?

Chapter 31

Lincoln

With no memory of the ride back to the clubhouse, I sat on my motorcycle waiting for Sid to appear. This morning's events continued to replay in my mind while I drew in several cleansing breaths, hoping to rid myself of the stench of betrayal. If I'd counted right, there had been fourteen rat bastards...nearly a third of the club's members. I shook my head and acknowledged Sid as his motorcycle pulled up next to me.

We'd agreed, with the remaining members, to close the club down until the dust settled. There was bound to be some fall out, and I wasn't sure if some wouldn't be stupid enough to keep from blabbing. Anything was possible, and the fact this had been brewing for years left too many uncertainties.

"Why'd you tell Mason to go home? We need to be ready for whatever comes next." Sid removed his helmet and sat foward on the tank as he removed his glasses and eyed me.

There were many reasons I'd told Mason to go home, but right then I didn't want to talk about them, so I didn't reply.

He let it be, and instead, asked, "Did I hear right? Is this all 'bout River?"

I took my own helmet off, giving myself a few seconds to rein back the temper that wanted to resurface. "It would seem so." I ground out through a clenched jaw. "My leadership is lacking 'cause of her. In Ned's opinion, she'd have been better off dead." I couldn't sit any longer, and I slung my leg off my motorcycle.

Sid released a low growl and his face was a mask of fury.

I paced in front of him, needing to know one thing. "Do you think I've let things slide?"

"Fuck no. You changed the direction of the club to protect River, and yeah, we don't fuckin' fight like we did, but our rep remains solid. I'll ask you a question. How many times in the last five years has a rival club come to show us who's boss?"

I stopped pacing to look him dead in the eye, and what I saw was no deception. It helped release a little of the strain knotting my shoulder muscles. "None."

"Exactly, and if Ned and the others had gotten their heads out of the past, they might have realized you've improved things. And yeah, as I said before, I worried it would change things. It did, but it's nice to be able to fuckin' sleep at night and not be waiting for someone to bust the door in."

The following chuckle was humorless, but I got the point he was making.

Sid leaned forward. "Let the dust settle and give it a few days to see what slides out of the woodwork." Color flooded his face and his gaze dropped to the tank as he carried on. "If I were you, I'd go and search out your man. He came today, no questions asked, and showed everyone what balls he had 'cause all he was worried 'bout was *you*." His voice thickened. "He's a rare find and you'd be a fool to let him go 'cause you feel you're not worthy of him—"

"What the fuck's that supposed to mean?"

"You're my brother in every sense, so I'm not gonna spell out your past. Just know that man loves you and today might have given him a big dose of reality, but remember this, he chose to stay." With that, Sid put his glasses back on, then his helmet. He nodded before starting his engine and taking off.

I returned to my motorcycle, and once back on it, I headed home, my head full of what Sid had said.

Distracted by the continued thoughts running through my head, I didn't initially hear River come into my work room. It had been three days since I'd told Mason to go home. I'd heard nothing from him, but I'd not reached out either.

"Poppy, I's had enough of dis nonsense. Ya been a grump for days and days. Ya needs to tell me what's wrong." Her tiny foot tapped on the floor as her hands went to her waist. Her face was so like Lizzie's when she got her mind made up, that a wave of emotion choked me and left me unable to respond.

The last client had left ten minutes earlier, so I used that as an excuse to keep myself occupied, clearing up for the day.

"Poppy, I's not playin'."

I glanced at her scowling face and crouched down. "I've a lot goin' on in my head—"

"Is this 'cause you and Mason had a fight?"

It was my time to scowl. "Who said we had a fight?"

Her finger wagged at me. "Don't take that tone with me. No one said anythin' but ya been going around snappin' and jumpin' down everyone's throat. And Mason says he's too busy to come and see me. Dat says ya had a fight."

I couldn't argue with her logic, but could you call radio silence an argument? Her eyes implored me to explain. I gave a heartfelt sigh and rubbed a hand down her ponytail. "We haven't had a fight, but things are a little tense right now." It was the best I could come up with, when I couldn't explain about what had happened on the weekend.

Things had returned to normal as if nothing had happened. It left a knot of tension at the base of my skull, reminding me daily that, at any minute, the sheriff could burst through the door.

The word was that Ned had regained consciousness the day before and had no memory of what had happened to him. He'd had a stroke that left his right side useless. Whether it was caused by the beating I'd given him, or his shitty lifestyle, who knew? But after what he'd done, he was lucky to still be breathing.

Doddie had a broken jaw that was wired shut so he couldn't talk. It seemed that Stevie had discharged himself from the hospital and hadn't been seen since. Riley and Beau were on an orthopedic ward with broken limbs, saying they'd fallen off their motorcycles. It looked like they'd gotten the message, but only time would tell. The other nine traitors had their patches stripped from them, and Sid had sent word out to other clubs we were on speaking terms with. He explained their treachery, just in case they went seeking entry to another club.

"—somethin' 'bout it, Poppy."

I tuned back in and caught the tail end of what River was saying and my heart leapt against my ribs at the smug look on her face. "What have you done, Spirit?" I got a sinking feeling when her gaze moved to the open door behind me and her face lit with a beaming smile.

"Hi, Mason," she sing-songed, giving me her answer.

Schooling my features, I stood and took a deep breath, hoping it would help my frantically beating heart as I turned to face Mason.

He was casually dressed in shorts and a T-shirt. His dark hair was swept back off his forehead. There were dark circles under his eyes that went with the deep grooves around his mouth. He looked so unhappy, I struggled not to go to him and wrap my arms around him. It was the wariness of his expression that held me back.

Had he come to tell me it was over? It was the kind of man he was. He'd have the courage to do it face to face. It was one of the many things I'd come to love about him. In the last three days, I'd thought about little else, especially with Sid's words ringing in my ears.

Yet the fear of rejection, of being too dark to his light left me doing fuck all. So I braced and gave a curt nod, hoping he'd get it over quick so that I could...what? Go on like he hadn't ripped out my heart?

"Hey, River. Could you give me and Poppy a minute alone?"

She skipped over to him and lifted her arms up. He bent immediately and lifted her up, allowing her to wrap her small arms around his neck.

"Ok, ya won't be long will ya? Ya promised me a picnic in the park, remember?" She kissed his cheek and whispered something in his ear I couldn't hear.

Did the offer of a picnic include me? A wild fluttering started in my stomach, until Mason's lips moved into a smile at whatever River was saying, that didn't reach his eyes. "We'll see, and yes, the basket is downstairs packed with goodies." He didn't meet my gaze as he lowered River. "Go on and get what you think you might need, and I'll be along in a minute."

She ran to the door not looking back. My hands balled at my sides when the door closed behind her. I hesitated. *Fuck it!* I closed the distance between Mason and me, his stiff posture not giving me any confidence that I was doing the right thing.

As if he'd made his mind up on something, his gaze met mine and his shoulders rolled back. "Tell me what happened."

I didn't pretend to not understand what the quietly asked question meant, and a part of me had known all along he'd ask. It was the way Mason was wired. He needed to understand everything, pick it apart so he could put it back together. I just wasn't sure if he'd want to do that this time, once he knew everything.

Chapter 32

Mason

There was a myriad of emotions crossing Linc's face and none of them gave me a good feeling. The last three days had been hell after he'd insisted I leave him to deal with the fallout. I'd gone home, albeit reluctantly, because I'd been furious at how he'd cut me out of what happened.

I'd done something I'd never done before and called in sick for work, needing to get my head together. To figure out what I wanted. Three days and what had it got me? A pounding headache and all but no sleep as I'd tried to work out what Linc's reasons were for nearly killing someone.

The more I'd thought about it, one thing had become clear; he'd never risk losing River. So that meant whatever had happened to make him lose it spoke to how serious this whole situation was for him. Late last night I'd taken my head out of my ass and come to a decision. If Linc wasn't going to reach out, then I needed to. Luis said I was the world's biggest stewer, that I could stew in my own misery for weeks, if not months, if something got to me. He wasn't wrong. I'd been doing that for years over not following in my father's footsteps.

One thing that had taught me was that I was the only one to suffer, so at two this morning, I'd hatched a plan. I needed to show Linc that the love I felt for him was real, and no matter what, I'd be there for him, until he got it through his thick skull.

Yet, when he remained silent and looking more closed off than ever, I had to forcibly hold myself still to stop the nerves from showing. Then I spoiled it by begging unashamedly, "Please. Talk to me."

He blew out a breath, then left me in a world of hurt as he explained only some, I was sure, of what had happened. I swallowed repeatedly as bile burned my chest and throat, wishing for five minutes alone with Ned after hearing that he had wished River had died at birth.

The anger in his voice was raw, and I could only imagine how he must have felt in that moment. To be betrayed because of a tiny defenseless child he'd chosen to stand up for and claim as his own.

I'd no clue what the outcome had been for Ned, and though I didn't wish him dead, a part of me wanted him to suffer for his misdeeds. It was wrong for Linc to take the law into his own hands, but I understood he wouldn't have gotten justice in court for what Ned and the others had tried to do to him. The tiny part of me that worried I'd misjudged Linc disappeared, even as nerves sprang to life with new worry. What jail time would Linc do for such a crime?

I didn't have time to think about it any further as he wrapped his arms around my waist and buried his face in my neck. He sucked in greedy breaths as my hands rose and stroked up and down his back.

"Did you kill him?" I whispered, the fear making it hard to speak. *Please let him say no, please let him say no.*

"He should be dead for what he did, but no." The deadly edge to his voice caused a shiver to race down my spine, and I was again reminded what this man could be capable of if someone he loved was threatened.

I sagged against him, my hands holding him tightly to me, needing the reassurance that he was safe.

Linc breathed out and our gazes met, and for the longest time we just started at each other. "I wanted to kill him. I wanted to wipe him off the face of the earth. Stamp him into the ground and piss on him. But there were two things stopping me. River...and you." His eyes fired with something potent—love.

It left me feeling giddy and light-headed as a hand moved to the nape of my neck and he claimed my mouth in a powerful kiss that was all about ownership. It was as if he were placing a searing brand into my skin as he claimed me.

All rational thought fled as he held me captive, his mouth doing delicious things to mine. The scent of his aftershave clung to his clothes and wafted around me. The arm behind my back tightened and all but lifted me against his body to grind his hard length against mine. We groaned in unison and I held on tighter, never wanting to let go.

Vaguely aware of a door opening, I tried to recall what I'd been about to suggest before Linc had kissed me.

"Poppy, put Mason down," River squealed in delight, and pulled me up short.

I sucked in several shaky breaths after prying my mouth off Linc's. I attempted to avoid looking at his flushed face and hooded eyes. Eyes that held promises of more to come later, if

I wasn't mistaken, that made my ass clench in anticipation. He clearly wasn't reading my face, that said he needed to behave if he didn't want to traumatize River any further.

"Why would I put Mason down, Spirit? He likes to be lifted up as much as you."

A wave of fierce heat spread up my neck, regardless of the heat pooling in my groin. "Fu...stop that."

Linc chuckled while River giggled.

"Good save, Mase," Linc stated as he finally let go, so I could step away from temptation.

I glanced down and noted my T-shirt was hanging over the front of my shorts, concealing my problem. The fucker in front of me had the audacity to give me a flirty wink before he crouched and concealed his own issue.

He flicked at River's ponytail. "So, is someone gonna tell me what the plan is for this evening? I'm pretty sure I heard mention of a picnic."

"We're going to have a picnic and watch a movie at the same time. Aren't we, Mason?"

"Absolutely, and we might even invite your Poppy. What do you think, River?" I gave her a not so subtle wink that made her giggle.

"I's had to put up with grumpy pants for days and days missin' ya, so I say let him come."

Linc coughed, and I laughed at the discomfort on his face at River's bluntness. "Is that right? We can't be havin' your Poppy grumpy now, can we?"

He attempted to give me a menacing scowl that fell way short with the humor glinting in his eyes. "I'll give you grumpy Poppy," he muttered, but he stood, and we followed an excited River upstairs so Linc could get changed.

We got to the drive-in early enough to get a spot near the front of the large screen, so River had a clear view from Linc's truck. She came and sat in the front while we ate from the picnic basket. It was only then that Linc asked what movie it was that we'd come to see.

River gave him the cutest grin, one I'd come to recognize when she'd maybe done something Linc might not be happy with, and my stomach dropped. Oh fuck! I'd been conned by a five-year-old. She'd assured me that Linc had promised her he was going to take her to see the old movie, *Grease*, from the late seventies.

She kept her big eyes on Linc. "It's *Grease*, Poppy."

My lips twitched at the resignation that crossed Linc's face before he glowered at me.

"Hey, don't look at me, she's your daughter." As I said it, a flicker of grief appeared before he could shield it.

I reached out and took hold of his hand, stroking it and letting him know I was there for him. His gaze softened and his fingers intertwined with mine.

"Yes, she is." There was a wealth of love in his words. "And she could be yours, too, if you'll have *us*?" This time his voice was barely more than a whisper, but the words rang loudly inside me as River shifted her attention to me.

Her expression was nearly identical to Linc's, full of nerves and expectation. A lump formed in my throat and my eyes ached with what they were both offering me.

I reached out the hand not gripping Linc's fingers painfully tight, to River and clasped her tiny one in mine, linking the three of us. I swallowed twice to unglue my tongue from the roof of my mouth.

"I'd no idea how taking your case would change my world. How it would teach me that even in the darkest place, light can be found if you look for it. That love can be more profound and unexpected in the best possible way. You both mean everything to me." I met Linc's gaze, so he understood what I was saying. "There is nothing I wouldn't do to protect my family, *nothing*."

A silent tear rolled down his cheek and my heart swelled as he took our joined hands and removed the tear.

"I know."

Those two words may not have been a declaration of love, but they were no less significant to a man who didn't trust, who'd been betrayed by those closest to him.

The screen in front of us lit up and broke the spell in the cab. I shifted River onto my lap, letting her snuggle into my body while I lay my head on Linc's broad shoulder.

"Let's watch the movie."

Epilogue

Six Months Later

Lincoln

The lovely dream I was having had me groaning in approval while I attempted to shove up into the wet heat surrounding my dick. There was a choked chuckle, and my eyes drifted open.

Not a dream.

Mason. When had he gotten here? He'd been away at some lawyer conference for the last three days and I hadn't expected to see him until tonight. My heart fluttered as it always did when he surprised me by returning home early, like he couldn't bear to be away from us.

Sunlight poured through the open curtains, blinding me as I looked down the bed at him between my thighs. Then his slippery tongue circled the crown of my dick and my eyes drifted shut at the immense pleasure making it impossible to think.

"Fuck...do that thing again with your tongue," I rasped.

Mason did as I asked while his hand crept up my chest toward my nipples. It took a second to register how close I was to coming when his fingers pinched hard and my balls ached with the need to come.

"I don't wanna come in your mouth, wanna come in your ass," I cried out as the tip of his tongue speared my slit, the pressure unreal.

When he showed no signs of giving up his prize, I bucked my hips. He coughed at the sharp jab to the back of his tonsils and released my dick. Only then did I lift one leg and roll fast to the other side of the bed. Twisting, I quickly grabbed for him and a second later, I had pinned him to the mattress.

His eyes twinkled with mischief. "Morning, sweetheart."

"I'll sweetheart you." I peppered his puffy lips with several kisses. "When did you get back?"

"About half an hour ago, I woke early and thought I could be doing something much better than lying in a cold hotel room, all alone." His mouth pressed against mine. "You don't mind that I decided to come home early, now do you?" He followed that up with a roll of his hips, causing his cock to rub against mine in a slow glide that left me panting.

The last six months had been full of ups and downs as we'd learned to navigate our relationship. Then, three months earlier, I'd started to resent him not being in my bed with me all the time when I'd reach out for him, only to wake and find the bed empty.

River had also been nagging over the prior months for me to ask Mason to move in permanently. Having never had a proper relationship before, or lived with someone I didn't class as family, I had no way of knowing if it was too soon. Yet as the days had gone by and the yearning had increased, I'd found myself taking the plunge.

I could still recall his face when I'd bumbled asking him.

As I watched Mason saunter naked toward the bathroom to go shower before he left me to return to his own home, the love I didn't often acknowledge crested so fast I thought I'd taken up surfing. "Move in with us," I blurted out and a surge of warmth flooded my face. Fucksake! What did you say that for!

He froze, his back toward me, making it impossible to see his reaction, although his body was doing a good job of saying I'd shocked him. It shuddered, and he swung around so fast, his cock whipped his leg. The look on his face was enough to get me up off the rumpled bed. He stood waiting as I walked to him and wrapped my arms around his sexy, warm skin. "You haven't answered me."

"Oh, thank you, God. Yes. Yes. You can't take it back," he muttered in between planting wet, hungry kisses against my lips.

Had he said yes?

I groaned, the answer seemingly less important when his tongue got busy sliding against mine as he deepened the kiss. His whole body rubbed against mine as he shuddered and moaned, "I love you."

"Where did you go?" Mason asked as our cocks bumped together, bringing me back to the present to remind me of how lucky I was.

I stared deeply into his eyes, seeing the love he offered so freely, and I dropped my forehead to his. "I was remembering asking you to move in with me," I answered honestly.

His eyes glowed and he slid his hands down to cup my ass cheeks. "Maybe we should re-enact what happened after I said yes. I think it involved you showing me whose bitch I was."

His warm breath touched my lips a second before he gave me a hungry kiss.

I blindly reached for the drawer holding the lube. We'd been tested months ago and no longer used a condom. And fuck had that been an eye opener, and why I often struggled to let Mason top when I knew how fucking unbelievable it felt to be inside his body with nothing separating us.

Lube dripped over the bed by the time he was begging to me to fuck him. Unable to resist his demands, I sunk into his willing body.

"Fuck, how you can still be this tight?" I panted against his mouth, willing myself to keep still and give him time to adjust.

"It's 'cause you got a giant co—"

I tilted my pelvis and rocked my dick against his prostate, and he shut up abruptly. Then he moaned so loudly I had to put a hand over his mouth.

I chuckled. "Shush, you'll wake River again."

His eyes widened, and I could see he'd recalled the last time River had burst through the door with her tiny baseball bat, thinking someone was hurting her Daddy. It was a moment I'd never forget. Mainly because of how weepy Mason got at River defending him, but it was also the first time she'd called him Daddy.

My throat thickened, and I lifted my hand from his mouth and replaced it with my lips. The emotions, that were as familiar to me as the tattoos on my chest, swelled inside me. "I love you," I murmured.

He moved, and one of his palms flattened against my chest, lying directly over my heart, his eyes sheening. "I know," he whispered.

Long moments I held his gaze as I slowly made love to the man who'd not only saved me, but who'd shown me there was more to life than just existing. Although it could be painful, the rewards meant I got to love this beautiful man, forever.

JP SAYLE

If you enjoyed this book read and would like to try something else by the author, read on for the first chapter in The Elves and the Bondage Daddy!

JP Sayle

JP Sayle

PROLOGUE

The king sat on the throne in front of me, a formidable scowl on his usually stunning face. It was a face that resembled my own. It should have done. He was my father after all. His face was twisted with a raw anger that caused the room to vibrate and my skin to hum unpleasantly. Gwilym, or Gwil to me, had been my best friend since birth and my boredom had yet again got us both into hot water. There was so little to do in the Elvedom that we had to make our own fun in order to keep us entertained.

"Why do I always have to repeat myself with you two? The last time you decided to have some fun, it took weeks to repair the damage to the palace, even with the use of collective magic."

The agitation in my father's voice forced me to keep a straight face. I did my best not to look over at Gwil, who stood next to me with his head bowed as Father berated us both again.

Why couldn't he understand that it was boring without making up games to play?

"Do you forget that as your father, I can read your thoughts, Benidic?" His silver brows merged into one straight line, his pale aqua eyes boring into mine. The strength of his magic made it impossible for me to move. "The games you play cause harm to others. You've become a thoughtless, spoiled brat and a nuisance to those who inhabit the palace." His gaze shifted to Gwil with a look of disappointment before moving back to me again. He sighed loudly.

The sound caused unease to unfurl in my stomach as he leaned back on his majestic throne. It glittered with the jewel colours of Elvedom. Our home was situated in a magical realm outside the earthly plane. A place that the earth dwellers had long since forgotten existed. The Elves created magic to protect the fabric of the earthly realm. The protector Elves worked day and night to ensure that the otherworld and other magical creatures had the magic needed to sustain life.

Those that dwelled in the magical realm never aged once they'd reached the age of maturity for Elves at three hundred earth years. I was still a long way off hitting maturity and those long eons stretched endlessly before me.

I eyed the jewelled throne that would one day be mine once Father decided I was ready, as his father had done, and his father before him, stretching back over the millennia. As the thought filled me with dread, I worked to shield my mind.

The Elvedom was filled with light and love. I, on the other hand, craved something more, something... a little darker. But with no experience beyond the realm, I had no idea what it was. So instead I created mayhem to fill the space inside me which felt empty and needy.

Father tapped a long, pale finger against his lips as they pursed. The unease inside me increased as his eyes narrowed. "I think I need to teach you both a lesson. One that shows the other Elves that I'm not going soft when it comes to the pair of you." He shifted forward, his long flowing robes of gold shimmering in the light. "Magic is a gift, and as such it should be treasured and not used for mischief. With that in mind,"—he lifted his hands, light shining from both palms as orbs floated above him—"from now on, your hands will only be able to create magic that assists others with no gain for either of you. I banish you to the earthly realm to fend for yourselves until you can prove that you are worthy to return."

My heart thumped against my ribs as Gwilym cried out, but it was already too late. The air moved around us, speeding so fast that my long silver tresses blew around my face. I reached for Gwil, gripping his hand as the world around us became a blur before simply disappearing. The reassuring sensation of Gwil's palm against mine kept me from crying out as panic seized my chest.

The world finally came back into focus but there was only darkness. I blinked rapidly, trying to see something. What was this?

In the Elvedom there was no darkness, only light.

When all I could see was an inky blackness that offered nothing, no light, no hope, an incessant buzzing started in my ears. I lifted my hand in an attempt to create light, releasing a cry when nothing happened. My father's words rang inside my mind. "Your hands will only be able to create magic that assists others."

"Oh, to the heavens! What have we done, Benidic?" Gwil cried out, the sound echoing. I twisted towards him, holding onto his hand as a lifeline.

Seconds passed, the darkness receding a little as my eyes began to adjust. I squeezed Gwil's hand harder. "We've messed up. Dear Elvedom, what are we to do? I know my father and he will not bring us back until he is satisfied that we have suffered." A shiver raced down my spine as

I inhaled an odd smell. "What is that awful stench?" I said through gritted teeth, doing my best not to open my mouth.

"It... it smells like rotten food," Gwil offered, inching even closer to me.

His warm body pressed against the length of mine, the fragrant scent of lavender taking the edge off my panic. I wrapped my arms around him and inhaled his scent. The weight of his body against mine was familiar due to the fact that we'd often shared a bed together growing up. His father was the head of the Elvedom protectors which gave him a place of honour in the Elvedom. Most of my memories included Gwil. We were both aware of our fathers' hopes that once we'd matured, we would mate and bond, as was customary of our kind. I loved Gwil like no other, yet there was something missing. Neither of us had spoken about it though, me because of my inner craving and him... well, I didn't know why he hadn't said anything.

To distract myself from the shivers racing down my spine, I recalled my history lessons about Earth.

"Look down there. Is that light? Maybe we can find someone to help us," Gwil exclaimed, not sounding at all convinced that that might happen.

I looked towards the light to see movement... people. Excitement pulsed to life, my fear decreasing. *The stories about humans showed that they could be kind.* The thought giving me hope, I propelled Gwil towards where the people were. I popped my head out to look around, Gwil whimpering and clinging to me.

The street lights showed dark grey floors and buildings made out of concrete and brick. Humans walked on the other side of the street, their clothes so different from our flowing robes.

I glanced down, my eyes widening at the dark trousers and thick coat which had replaced my silk trousers and robe. It was only then that I registered that Gwil wore something similar to me. "It would appear Father has thought of everything," I said, the reality that we wouldn't be going home any time soon, sinking in.

"But what are we going to use as coin to buy the things we need?" Gwil fretted as he dug his hands into every pocket in the clothes he could find, coming up empty every time.

"We'll think of something. We have to." Tears clogged my throat as I tugged Gwil towards me. "We're going to be fine, you'll see. All we need to do is find someone to help with our magic and we'll be home in no time." I added, putting as much conviction into my voice as I could, Gwil's eyes sheening with tears. "You'll see, I promise."

I just prayed to the Elves of the otherworld that I could keep my promise.

JP Sayle

JP SAYLE

BOOKS BY THE AUTHOR

Standalone
When Fake Changed Everything
Christmas beyond Christmas
The Elves and the Bondage Daddy (Grim and Sinister Delights Book 5)

Series
The Potters Creek Series
A Christmas Wish (book one)

The App Series
The App: Daddy kink (book one)
The App: Littles (book two)
The App: Puppy play (book three) - December 2020

The Flamingo Bar Series
Always More (book one)
The Little Side of Me (book two)
3 is the magic number (book three) - January 2021

La Trattoria Di Amore Series
Puzzle Pieces (book one)
Dominated but not Subdued (book two)

JP SAYLE

The Playroom Series
Mine, Body and Soul: Part One
Mine, Body and Soul: Part Two
Mine, Body and Soul: Part Three
Ferron's Journey: Damaged Part One (book four)
Ferron's Journey: Hidden Part Two (book five)
Ferron's Journey: Revelation Part Three (book six)
Mine, Body and Soul Trilogy
Ferron's Journey Trilogy

The Billionaire Playground Series
Property of a Billionaire (Book one)

The Manx Cat Guardians Series
Where it all Began: Origins (Book 1)
Seeing Beyond the Scars (Book 2)
Destiny Collides Past and Present (Book 3)
Searching for a Soul to Love (Book 4)
The 12 Disasters of Christmas (Book 5)
Laws of Attraction (Book 6)
The Teacher's Boy (Book 7)
Boxset

JP Sayle

Audio Books
Mine, Body and Soul, Part One: The Playroom Series
Mine, Body and Soul, Part Two: The Playroom Series
Mine, Body and Soul, Part Three: The Playroom Series
Daddy Kink: The App (book one)
Always More: The Flamingo Bar (book one)
When Fake Changed Everything
Ferron's Journey: Damaged Part One
Ferron's Journey: Hidden Part Two

JP Sayle

JP Sayle

ABOUT THE AUTHOR

Hi all,

My name is Jayne and I live in the Isle of Man. A tiny place in the Irish sea. It's an island steeped in folklore and history and just begs to have stories written about it, and one of my first inspirations. Over the last few years that has changed and now I find inspiration everywhere.

I'm an eclectic kinda girl so I've written contemporary and historical gay romance with a paranormal twist, daddy kink, fake boyfriends, out for you and enemies to lovers. My head is so full of ideas. I never know where it will take me next. I had a twelve book plan for 2020 and I smashed it and will release fourteen books and already I've a few new ones bubbling inside me waiting to be written ☺

I hope you have enjoyed this book, and if you are in need of more, then you can find all my other books, on Amazon and in KU.

If you're interested in keeping up to date with what I'm planning then why don't you follow and join me on the following links.

JP Sayle

You can find me and follow me on:

Newsletter Sign up

Goodreads

Tumblr

Bookbub

Instagram

Twitter

Facebook

Website address

Facebook Author page

JP Manx Minx's

Patreon

If you would like to give me any feedback or just have any questions, go ahead and friend me on Facebook, and I would be happy to answer anything. Well, almost anything. I hope you enjoyed this book as it was a little different for me. If you would also like to leave a review, then I would love to read your thoughts.

JP Sayle

Thank you for taking the time to be part of my dream.

JP Sayle

Printed in Great Britain
by Amazon